Led to Water

Led to Water

By Laura Christian

RAMBLING RHODESY
PUBLISHING

DEDICATION

For all the adult children who have removed themselves from the lives of their parents or relatives, I support you. Always put on your own "mask" first before helping others.

I hope you find peace as you turn over your new leaf.

Thank you to everyone who supported me in writing this book.

Thank you to Brentley Gore, whose music inspired me to write this story. If you don't know his music, check out this book's playlist.

BONUS

Listen to some of the music that inspired this book.

Scan the QR code below.

ONE

"**M**OTHERFUCKER!"

The word rang out like a shot echoing through the trailer park as Analese crashed to the ground.

She sighed heavily, staring at the cloudless sky above her. It stared back, blue and mocking, as she cursed again. She wanted to throw a full-blown tantrum, but her back and hips hurt too much from the impact to exercise her frustration any other way than a litany of curses that would have impressed even a sailor.

With a deep exhalation, she pulled herself up to her knees, then threw her ass in the air and finally managed to get her creaky body into a standing position. She started to dust off her pants when she noticed a deep gash through the four-inch rip in her jeans soaking with blood.

"Oh, well, this is just lovely. Perfect! Fucked me again, Mom, for posterity." The ground below her was littered with shattered bowls and a bottomless cardboard box. When the bottom had come loose, she'd lost her balance and in trying to save the items, ultimately tripped down the stairs and landed in her current position.

"It couldn't have happened to a nicer set of fifty-year-old mixing bowls," she grumbled. She didn't know why she was talking to herself. But at least she was letting the frustration out instead of holding it in.

Ever since she'd gotten the call two months ago about her mother's passing, an emotional pit had been growing inside her. All the pent-up incidents she had tried to forget came creeping back one at a time. The lies. The manipulation. The gaslighting. So many specific things and so many unresolved feelings.

"Tonight at dinner, you're going to help me convince your dad to buy me a handheld TV. So, you're going to say..."

"Girls only get their periods if they've had sex. So, if

you have sex, I'll know."

"We can only do this when Dad's not home."

"Boys only want sex out of girls. Don't trust them."

"Your dad and I never have sex. He doesn't love me because I'm fat."

"When I get to heaven, I'm going to sit on Jesus' knee, and He's going to tell me stories."

"You look like a sex pot."

As she stood in the middle of the barren "front yard" of her mother's trailer lot collecting broken pieces of bowls, she didn't know what a "sex pot" even was. And she had spent a great deal of her life trying to figure it out. What she had grasped from her mother was that men were all evil scum and only wanted to ravish women. Sex was also evil and should be avoided. Wouldn't she be proud to know that at forty-two, Analese had kept her cherry?

She had been on the verge of exploding since she got the news of her mother's "untimely" demise, and then she got the call from the trailer park where her mother had been roosting for the last decade. The park had threatened to either sell it or slap her, as the daughter, with a host of fees that she couldn't

3

begin to touch. She hoped she could sell the piece of junk and break even on the park's demands. But to do that, she had to assess the property and clear out the debris.

She hadn't spoken to the woman in nearly twenty years. When her parents divorced after thirty years of marriage, she was thrilled. Maybe there would be peace. Instead, what ensued was a divisive battle to make her children choose between their parents.

Which led her to this moment, bleeding with a box of broken dishes at her feet. There was something poetic about it in the darkest sense.

Analese took a fortifying breath and returned to the trailer for a trash bag to collect the refuse. She wondered if she should simply shove everything out the front door and collect it in trash bags. It was unlikely there was anything of value outside of a stray coin.

She needed every penny she could get, and the frugal side of her cautioned that she shouldn't judge what someone else might consider to be treasure in her mother's stash. If she could make $100, it would be worth it. Grimly, the thought crossed her mind that she might have to live in this dump. Maybe because it was an inheritance, the park would allow her to stay despite not being old enough to live in the elder community.

"Stop it, Analese. Stop thinking and work." She had promised herself she would at least fill her car to the gills with anything worth keeping and donate anything she couldn't sell, like clothing and dishes, before she stopped for the day. The rest she was going to put into a tiny storage locker. When it was finished, she was planning a yard sale to see what her mother's life had amounted to. And if she scrubbed very hard, maybe she could have enough money to sustain herself till she could find a job.

Overwhelmed at the thought, she slumped to the front steps that she had so recently fallen down and pressed her head to her knees.

Her life had exploded. First came the dead mother, then came the stock market crash, which had reduced her savings to a few hundred dollars, and the day she had gone to ask for a leave of absence to clean up the mess, she'd been laid off.

She was well into a crying jag when she heard the

sound of a vehicle braking nearby. It sounded like a jalopy from the groaning of the door opening then slamming shut with a metallic clank.

"Hey, you okay?" a male voice called out from the street.

Analese did not lift her head till she heard the sound of footsteps out front.

"Miss?" the voice asked again.

As she lifted her eyes, she saw a man roughly her age approaching. He was rail thin, gaunt-faced, and his ponytail looked a little greasy as it brushed his neck. But he was tall — well over six feet, she thought as she appraised him.

"I'm fine," she replied, both hands sliding across her cheeks to remove the tears. She hoped to God she didn't have snot running down her face as well, and she scrubbed at it with the back of her sleeve. Which was stupid, she told herself because wet-faced or not, there was no way to hide her red eyes or the fact that she'd been sitting on the steps of a trailer park house crying like a runaway.

The man stopped a few feet away, scratching the back of his neck awkwardly. He pointed with the

6

other hand at her leg.

"The blood sorta says otherwise."

Analese laughed in surprise. At least he hadn't indicated her ugly cry face. She followed his gesture to see that the blood had soaked down her shin, creating a horror movie effect.

"Oh. That."

"I'm no doctor, but I have a sneaking feeling that you might need some stitches," he suggested.

There was the slightest tinge of a Southern drawl in his voice curving the sounds in the words "I'm" and "might." The accent lent some actual concern to his words, and she studied the wound further. It was still weeping, but it didn't seem like a lot. Her bloody pantleg was telling a different story.

"There's an urgent care not far. I can give you a ride," he offered. "I don't mind."

"Oh, I can take myself," she replied, reaching for the phone in her back pocket. She held her phone aloft to show him she could look it up herself. The shattered screen nearly cut her fingers as she did so.

"Are you fucking kidding me?" she yelled.

The man seemed to think this was funny, and he

laughed. It was a short bark, but the smile that lingered on his face was infuriating. He bridged the distance between them and held out a hand.

"Come on. It's your lucky day. I'll chauffeur you to the urgent care *and* the phone store."

Every instinct in her fought accepting his help. He could be an axe murderer. She looked past him to his truck. It wasn't the rusted-out mess she'd expected. Instead, it was a white work truck, freshly clean but for the fresh mud kicked up by the tires on the otherwise pristine surface. It did look at least twenty years old. The passenger door proclaimed it belonged to "Boris Brothers Maintenance Services."

With a sigh, Analese took his hand and stood. Just inside the door was her purse, and she'd absolutely need her wallet to go anywhere, regardless of who was driving. She slung the long strap over her shoulder and started toward the truck.

The man wasn't following. "Don't you want to lock up?" he asked.

Analese looked from him to the open trailer door. The black trash bag was wilted next to the stoop, and all she could see inside was hazy golden light and piles of plastic grocery bags in various stages of disintegration. She shrugged.

"Who'd want to steal anything in there?"

He scratched his neck again. "That could be the blood loss talking." He held out a hand. "I'll lock up, so you don't have to take the stairs."

Indifferent, she pulled the keys from her pocket to deposit in his palm.

"Sure. Thanks."

She didn't bother to watch as he jangled them, and his footsteps sped into a jog. She heard the distinct sound of shoes on wooden stairs and the repeated slam of the door. By that time, she had reached the truck. It was locked, so she turned and leaned her backside against it to watch him trot back to her.

"It's not about theft. It's just meanness. Dumb kids get in there and burn it down, it'll be worse than theft," he explained, handing her back the keys.

"Maybe. Or maybe the insurance money would be easier than cleaning it up," she countered.

"Did she have insurance?" he asked, unlocking the passenger door and holding it open for her.

"Oh." Analese mulled the thought over. When he slipped into the driver's side, she stared at him openly. "I take it from that statement that you knew her?"

He twisted his mouth as he started the engine. "Yes. I've spent some time there."

Her nose wrinkled. "What kind of time?"

"Fixing toilets, sinks, pretty much all the plumbing. And a variety of other issues."

She sighed in relief. "Right. Maintenance services. Are you Boris or Brother?"

"Neither. Dalton." He glanced at her as they waited at the stop sign at the mouth of the Ashford Pines Elder Trailer Park Community. "So how did you know Mary?"

Analese wanted to throw another tantrum, but she also wasn't sure she wanted to open up to this stranger. It was bad enough she was bleeding all over his clean vehicle. He didn't need to delve into a therapy session about her crappy childhood.

"I'm her daughter," she stated.

"Ana?" he balked. "She talked about you all the time."

She looked at him. "I'm so sorry."

He laughed. "I was expecting horns, stilettos and a G-string. Maybe a tail."

Shrugging, she turned back to the passing scenery.

"You don't look anything like a heathen," he complimented.

"Well, thank you for that. I'm also not a lesbian," she added. "Despite my very masculine shoes."

Dalton glanced from the road into the passenger side floorboard. "Good to know," he replied.

Analese liked his answer. If he had spent any time with her mother, he wouldn't be surprised by the wild accusations her mother liked to make. Anyone who knew Mary for any length of time figured her out.

"She accused me of that when I was fourteen," she explained.

He smiled kindly. "She had some interesting opinions."

"You're a saint for helping her."

"It's not like I did it out of the kindness of my heart. I got paid," he expounded.

"Small consolation," she mumbled.

They were quiet for a moment, and Analese began to wonder what Dalton thought the word "close" meant.

Two

I**T WAS ONLY ANOTHER MINUTE** before he clicked on his blinker and turned into the parking lot of a small building cobbled together with leftover paneling and concrete blocks. Milk chocolate brown paint covered every last inch of the exterior, except where it was flaking off to reveal school bus yellow underneath.

"This is the urgent care?" she asked.

He shrugged. "They're clean inside," he admonished. "Round here, you can't judge a book by its cover."

Dalton was, of course, right. When she walked inside, the décor might have been outdated, but everything was clean, right down to the asbestos tiles that reminded her of elementary school. They gleamed with fresh wax, and everything smelled a little bit citrusy to mask the bleach.

The bell that had tinkled above the door when she entered brought a nurse rushing to the front desk to offer aid.

"Oh, dear," the woman chirped. "Don't even sit down, honey. Come this way, and I'll bring you the paperwork."

The nurse was at least fifty pounds overweight, and her loose scrubs jiggled around her as she rushed to let Analese into one of the exam rooms behind the counter.

"You got insurance, darlin'?"

"Yes," she answered, then began running the calculations in her head. Her insurance was good for thirty days, but only twenty-three had passed since she'd been laid off. If she was going to need medical attention, at least she'd managed to squeeze it in before her coverage ended.

She hobbled past the nurse holding the door for her with a nod of thanks.

"Dalton, what happened?" the nurse called.

"At the trailer park. I found her this way," he explained, holding up both hands. "I just gave her a

14

ride. I'll wait here." He dropped into one of the waiting room chairs, stretching his long legs out in front of him and crossing at the ankles.

The nurse got Analese settled into a room and returned with the paperwork. "I'll need your ID and your insurance card. If you can fill out some information here and here." She pointed to several spots on one page. "I can fill out the rest. And you'll need to sign the disclosure papers, too. We'll get you on your way in no time."

Analese had already filled out her name and was working on the medical history tick boxes. "Wow. I should get hurt more often around here. You make it so easy."

The woman chuckled. "I'm going to make some copies. I'll be back."

Analese continued filling in blanks, cringing when she got to the employer section. With a heavy heart, she filled in her former employer's information. By the time her nurse returned, she had set the clipboard on the tiny counter and was peeling back the denim around her knee to see the damage.

"Davidson?" the nurse perked up. "Any relation to

Mary Davidson?"

Fighting the urge to groan, Analese sat up straight and quit picking at her knee. "Yes. She was my mother."

The nurse frowned, touching her good knee with three fingers. "I am so sorry for your loss," she offered. "We all knew Mary. Had a lot of little problems."

Analese smiled tightly at her, folding her hands in her lap and squeezing her fingers together calmly.

"Thank you," she replied. "We weren't close."

"We know. But you still lost a parent, and someday, that might hurt." She gave Analese a friendly smile and passed back her cards. "I'll tell Dr. Reese you're here and get Nancy to come take your vitals."

A young nurse in dark blue and grey scrubs nearly collided with the front desk nurse in the doorway.

"Hi, I'm Nancy," she introduced. Without another word, she flitted around the office, gathering tools and setting them on the edge of the counter near the exam table. Scissors, tape, gauze, a small pink plastic tray, tweezers, and so forth. None of it was shocking.

When Nancy the baby nurse turned with scissors in hand, Analese did not expect the next step to be cutting her jeans from the ankle up the side of her leg to two inches above the tear.

"What are you doing?" she shrieked. But of course, it was too late now. There was a jagged cut running along the inseam, and the real horror began when the scissors slipped through the fabric across her thigh.

"Oh, it's standard practice. We have to cut away the material."

"Couldn't I have taken them off? Nothing's broken."

The nurse shrugged. "We have to cut them to prevent further damage to the area."

Analese started to cry as the nurse completed the task, and she looked down at the uneven slice through her pants. The other full leg mocked her, and she lay back on the bed and sobbed.

Dr. Reese was probably wonderful, but Analese barely noticed. He patted her shoulder when he arrived, describing how gentle he was going to be treating her wound.

She had only brought the one pair of jeans with her. Back at the mobile home park, she had a pair of shorts, but those were all the bottoms she'd packed! And with her budget so tight, a new pair of pants was not in her future. She supposed she could root through her mother's clothing to look for something, but that thought was even more depressing than walking around in one-legged jeans.

There was a numbing spray and about three tink-tink-tinks of debris landing in the plastic kidney shaped bowl that Nancy the horrible seamstress had set out. Then came the debridement which sent a sluice of bloody, muddy water cascading down her calf and over her sock and shoe. Four stitches followed, and then the gauze was wrapped, and she was ready to go. Minus a pant leg.

"Good as new. Looks like you fell?" the doctor questioned.

Analese sat up and nodded, grateful when he held out a box of tissues.

"Whenever you're ready, meet Dottie at the front desk, and she'll get you checked out. If you have any pain still in about three or four days, or if you bleed through the dressing, you come back and see us, okay?"

"Yes, sir," she agreed.

She gave herself a moment before drying her face and washing her hands at the tiny exam room sink before exiting to pay the bill. She couldn't bear to look at the good Samaritan who'd brought her in as she began her walk of shame.

Twenty-five dollars later, she made the inevitable turn to face Dalton.

Wisely, he said nothing, standing to hold the door open for her. They remained silent all the way to the truck. It wasn't until they were on the road again that she spoke.

"I appreciate you taking me. They did four stitches."

He cringed. "I thought it looked like a few. Too much blood for a wait-and-see wound."

"I guess you see a lot of those in your line of work."

"More than I'd like." He held his right hand out toward her, cocking his thumb to the side. "Three stitches mending a fence."

Analese could see a faint white scar with three holes on either side. "Looks like very long division," she teased.

He chuckled. "You still okay for the phone store?"

She groaned. "I'd already forgotten about that." She looked down at her legs. "I look like a clown. Do you think they'll take pity on me and give me a discount since I am clearly wounded?"

"Anything is possible."

She sighed, picking the fabric at the edge of the jagged cut along her thigh.

"You could cut the other leg off and call 'em shorts."

"That's actually not a bad idea. If I had a pair of scissors, that would be stellar."

"You really are having a lucky day. First a chauffeur, and now a handyman who happens to have a pair of pretty heavy-duty scissors in a little toolbox under the passenger seat."

"You do not!" she balked, reaching down below the seat. She felt around finding a paper straw wrapper, a flashlight, and then a shallow metal box, which she pulled free. It was only about three inches deep, holding a hammer, a few screwdrivers, allen keys, and an adjustable wrench. And as promised, a pair of orange-handled copper-bladed scissors.

"It's my quick fix kit," he explained. "I'll even keep my eyes on the road like a gentleman while you work."

"My hero," she drawled.

"But we're almost there, so…don't dawdle," he warned. "I'll even try not to hit any potholes."

She gave him a thumbs up while evaluating how to get started, then made quick work of the extra pant leg. It was awkward trying to cut across the top of her thigh and even worse doing the back side, but she managed, evening out the wounded leg as well.

"It's not anywhere close to perfect, but it beats the work Nurse Hatchet did," she grumbled as she put his scissors back in the kit and stowed it beneath her seat.

He snorted. "I'm going to drop you at the phone store and come back and get you in about twenty minutes. That okay with you?"

She nodded. "I'm so sorry to be wasting all of your day," she apologized, folding up the denim leftovers.

"Neh, I'm self-scheduled," he replied. "I don't mind."

He dropped her at the store and waited to pull away till she had entered the building. The salesperson was sympathetic, but the best they could offer was a similar refurbished phone. The financial hit was far worse than the damaged knee, but she needed a phone if she was going to make all the required arrangements and drive back home.

When she climbed back in Dalton's truck and found he'd brought her a giant foam cup of lemonade, she nearly devolved into tears again.

"Thank you," she mumbled, greedily sucking the sweet liquid through the straw. She hadn't realized how thirsty she was.

He held up a small bottle of ibuprofen as well. "You've had a rough day, despite all my heroics. Thought you could use a little pick-me-up."

Tears rolled over her cheeks as she accepted the item.

"You shouldn't have," she croaked, then started laughing and crying at the same time.

Dalton joined her as he pulled away from the

store. "I would *not* buy a lotto ticket today if you do that sort of thing," he cautioned. "In fact, maybe find a couch to lay on and don't move till morning."

She chuckled as she poured four pills out of the bottle and slurped them down with the lemonade. "I'm not sure. In mom's place, it feels like there's likely some danger of something on the couch or any surface for that matter."

"If you can make it to the morning, things will get better," he comforted. "You always get a fresh slate when the sun rises."

The thought was soothing, and she sipped her lemonade quietly until they reached the trailer park and he stopped in front of her mother's run-down abode.

"Thank you for everything," she offered.

"It's what I do — fix broken things." He cut the engine and reached to unbuckle his seat belt. "Go rest. I'll come check on you in the morning and make sure nothing's devoured you in the night. I don't have a job scheduled till afternoon tomorrow."

She wanted to tell him she'd be fine. However, since she'd arrived three days ago, this was the first breath of fresh air she'd had. The first time she hadn't wanted to throw things as each item she unearthed tore open more traumatic memories. Maybe seeing him again would be a silver lining.

She nodded resolutely. "I will even attempt to make coffee if you like," she offered.

"I've seen her coffee maker. Pass. Besides, I'm not sure you should be allowed around boiling liquids if today was any indication."

"Don't worry," she sassed. "I'll use my tail for balance." She hopped out of his pickup with more spring than she expected to have and collected her cup and fabric. "Thank you again. I owe you."

He tipped an invisible hat to her, exiting the vehicle as well and locking it before walking across the lot to a mobile home two doors down.

THREE

ANALESE NEARLY FELL OFF THE couch when she heard a knock at the trailer door the following morning. After Dalton had dropped her off, she'd cleared the junk mail off the couch to have a place to rest and wound up finding two and a half crusty blankets stuck to its surface beneath the junk. The half blanket smelled like cat pee, and she worried that she might unearth a skeleton before it was over.

The half blanket she'd thrown out the door. The other blankets she'd washed and dried to cover up the couch to have place to sit. By the time she had made the couch usable, she had no choice but to follow Dalton's advice and rest. She had passed out cold sorting mail into trash and overdue bills only to be woken by what was inevitably his knock.

"What time is it?" she grumbled, reaching for her cell and stumbling toward the door. Her knee throbbed already, and her stomach growled like a caged animal. It was nearly 9 a.m.!

Dalton was waiting on the porch patiently.

"I'm so sorry. I haven't slept this late since I was a teenager," she explained.

He waved her off, pressing past her with a plastic bag. "You had a big day yesterday. Sleep was probably the best thing you could've done."

Analese's stomach let out a series of rumbles as she smelled hot food emanating from the bag.

"Wow! I've never seen the tabletop before," he noted, pulling out one of the chairs and setting the bag on its surface. "How long have you been here?"

"Four days today. Got in late Friday. I think that's why I fell yesterday morning. I'm feeling a little overwhelmed."

He looked around slowly and nodded. "I can see that." He peeled open the bag, pulling out a pair of foam takeaway boxes, setting one across the table and the other in front of himself. He extended a plastic-wrapped set of silverware with a napkin, salt and pepper.

"Maybe if you start out your day right, there will

be no more trips to the urgent care," he suggested.

She plopped down in the chair opposite him, poking one of the utensils through the sealed end. Extracting the fork, she opened the lid to find six triangles of beautifully arranged homemade-looking French toast. In the well to the side were two strips of bacon and a few pieces of cut fruit. She inhaled the heavenly scent and nearly choked on the resulting saliva that filled her mouth then dug in without pretense.

The first bite evoked an obscene groan, and she covered her mouth with a chuckle as she chewed slowly and swallowed.

"What do I owe you for this?" she mumbled.

"Nothing. You paid in porno groans," he teased.

She snorted. "That's a thing?"

He shrugged. "People are buying feet pictures on the internet. I bet you could've earned a lot more than breakfast with that one."

She nodded, slicing off another bite and dipping it in the syrup cup. "You are a wealth of knowledge."

"Just trying to help," he replied. His eyes roamed the kitchen. "How are you getting through this? It's a lot for someone not close."

She pondered the question before answering. "You'd think it would be easier being estranged."

He shook his head. "Estranged isn't the same as being a stranger."

She arched a brow. "Sounds like someone with experience."

"Maybe." He stuffed his mouth with an entire triangle of French toast. His jaw worked slowly, barely keeping syrup from dripping down his lips.

Analese fought a laugh and reached for a piece of bacon. She gestured to the couch behind him. "I passed out sorting mail last night. Overdue bills and coupons that expired six years ago."

Gulping down his oversized bite, he waved the black plastic fork around. "Having an objective eye might speed things up if you're interested," he offered.

"Why Boris or Brother, are you offering your services? You might be out of my price range."

He reached for his paper coffee cup and turned it with his fingertips. "What is your budget?"

"Exactly what the little boy shot at. Zero."

"Oh!" he sighed in relief. "Well, good. That's exactly what my services are worth."

She narrowed her eyes. "Before I accept, I feel like I should absolutely know more about you. You are far too nice. You're a closet serial killer, aren't you?"

"If I was, I must be very bad at it for you to figure it out so fast."

She shook her head, spearing a strawberry. "I knew it yesterday on the way to urgent care. Axe murderer."

He shrugged, waving one hand from side to side in the air. "Will a hatchet do? I don't usually have an axe on my person."

"I'm going to feel a little cheated, but okay," she acquiesced.

After a moment, he shoved half a slice of bacon in his mouth, chewed, then swallowed. "Now, you not knowing anything about me isn't entirely true. You know I live nearby; you know where I work; you know my name; and you know that I didn't murder your mother no matter how many times she told me how much more respectable I'd be if I cut my hair."

Analese snickered. That did sound like her mother. On this point, she didn't necessarily disagree, but she would never admit it.

He leaned on one elbow and narrowed one eye to point at her with his fork. "All I know about you is your relation to Mary and that you're clumsy with a box of heavy dishes on an uneven staircase. For all I know, *you* could be an axe murderer."

"Well, if I was, I would've started with Mom, so clearly I'm not."

Dalton made quick work of his bacon and fruit, closing the lid on his takeaway container and pressing it back into the plastic grocery bag.

"So are you going to give me details?" he asked. "Or do I need to waterboard you?"

Analese barked out a laugh. She hadn't realized how much she'd missed having a friend. "Which details?"

"I don't know. How 'bout a fair trade? Where do you work?"

"Well, to be honest…I'm unemployed as of about three weeks ago."

Dalton's face went slack for a moment before his

eyebrows shot into his hairline. "Oh. I stepped in that pile of . . . garbage, didn't I?"

She shrugged. "No. It's a legit question. It's still a little fresh for me. But I guess the silver lining is that I was able to drive here with unlimited time."

"Where did you drive from?"

"Indiana. I'm in South Bend."

He nodded. "How far was that?"

"A hard eight hours or so with stops."

"So you're a road warrior," he cited.

"No," she clarified. "I'm cheap. There are twenty-four hours in a day. It's one-third of a day. I might be over forty, but I'm not dead yet." She closed her container, nothing left but a few dregs of syrup in the cup. Embarrassed that he might think she was a pig, she shoved the container into the bag with his. At least she could give the semblance of having some restraint. But she had been hungry after living on leftover ramen and canned goods that still looked viable in the pantry.

He tied a knot in the bag and stood. "Do you have something specific you'd like to do that requires more than one person?"

"I need to get rid of the furniture, but I can't even get to it. And until I'm ready to actually sell, I can't get rid of all of it."

He scanned the space. "I vote for getting the garbage out first. We can throw it in the back of the truck, and I'll drop it off on the way home tonight."

"That's too much. At least let me go with you so I can help unload."

He narrowed his eyes, lips puckering as he looked skyward. "Let's see how much there is by the time I have to go, and we can reassess then."

"Deal," Analese replied.

Dalton opened the door, pinning it back to let the daylight and fresh air in, then stepped out to toss the trash bag beside the stairs.

"We'll pile it here to start with, then take it all at once," he instructed.

With a plan, the pair worked in tandem, punctuating the time when they found something particularly gross or interesting like the half bag of cat food that was covered with ants and contained a small family of mice. Analese was especially grateful for Dalton's help when he took care of it without so much as a squeak. Even more amazing was how he returned with a container of bug spray to kill off the remaining colony of ants once the bag had been removed.

"That cat has been dead for three years," Dalton commented as he proceeded to scoop out the dead insects with a wad of paper towels. "I only met it once. I don't remember its name. But poor thing was terrified, and I caught it crawling under the couch when I came in."

"How do you do it? Working with people when they're horrible and hoarders?"

He shrugged. "Everyone, even Mary, when I'd do something for her or say something kind…at least for a minute…is happy. And if I can give that to someone that didn't have it, I have the greatest job in the world."

The words resonated with her for a long moment as she pulled spices out of the pantry and tossed them into the trash bag arranged in the sink.

"That's a really cool way to think about it."

"It's like a game," he expounded, tossing a bag out the front door onto the growing pile. "It's why I'm pretty much the only guy that gets the jobs in this community. Money isn't the only thing that makes it rewarding."

Her insides quivered at the statement. She thought of his rescue the previous day. It had been completely unexpected, but she'd thought of his utter kindness the whole evening afterward. Without his aid, she could've suffered more than a ruined pair of pants.

"Thank you for yesterday and today in case I haven't said it. I've been thinking it."

He nodded. "Glad to feel useful," he answered, then disappeared with a bag of garbage. She reached for the jars in the very back of the cabinet, wondering how her short mother had gotten them in there in the first place. She closed her fingers around the very last one with a sigh of relief.

She heard Dalton outside. "Hey, Martin."

A deep voice answered. "Dalton. Whatcha doin' at Mary's place?"

"Lending a hand. Have you met Mary's daughter?"

"No, I haven't."

She heard footsteps approaching and groaned. She was in no state to meet anyone with grime all over her arms and legs wearing the same cutoff jeans from the day before and a gauze-wrapped knee.

An older, white-haired man poked his head inside, his pocked red nose covering a large portion of his face. The bill of his hat brushed the doorway.

"You Ana?" he grumbled.

She climbed down the step ladder and brushed her hands on her hips. "Yes, sir. Analese."

"Martin," he replied. He craned his neck around, taking in the interior. "Got your work cut out for you. Your mom was a piece of work."

"Yes, sir. She was," Analese agreed. "I'm working hard to meet your deadline. I'm not sure how long it will take to sell the place, though."

"Well, I see what you're up against. We can work something out if you get it fixed up real nice. But I see you've already found Dalton, so that's a good sign." He tapped his knuckles against the door frame. "I won't keep ya. Just wanted to see what was happening at old Mary's place."

Analese was glad she had climbed down, or she

certainly would've fallen again. Every conversation she'd had with Martin by phone was unreasonable. His offer to work something out was completely uncanny. If she hadn't heard Dalton call him by name, she wouldn't have believed it.

"I'd appreciate that. I'm planning to leave it empty. I wouldn't trust the furniture to help sell it."

He made a moue of consideration. "Leave the table and chairs. Chuck the rest." He pulled away with a half wave, and Analese scrambled after him, trying not to trip over the piles.

"Martin, I was wondering what the rules are about having a yard sale here."

"I don't like 'em," he replied. "Brings in the riff-raff. But it's hard to say no when somebody dies. When you're ready, let's talk again." Martin turned his back and rambled down the stairs. He patted Dalton on the shoulder. "You'll get to that water heater in Gerry's place today?"

"Yes, sir," Dalton answered with a firm nod. "He asked me to come after one."

"Gettin' close," Martin noted, then toddled away, pulling up his baggy trousers on one side and letting the other remain a peep show.

Carefully, Analese made her way down the steps to stand close enough to Dalton that she could keep her voice low.

"He is an enigma," she murmured.

"Wrapped in a mystery," Dalton added.

"He was a total butthole about this whole thing when he notified me about Mary's trailer."

For a moment, there was silence between them as they watched Martin climbing the stairs to another residence.

Dalton spoke first. "I've been working here a while. And in a community like this, there's a lot of turnover. People don't usually end up here 'cause they've lived great lives. And there's a lot of deadbeat kids and relatives," he explained, then glanced at his watch. "He's right. It's after noon. We've got just enough time to load up."

She glanced at the growing pile. "Why don't you wash up and go on. I'll take care of it."

He hefted a bag in each hand. "Nope. You want Martin on your good side; bring a bag."

Analese opened her mouth to protest, but felt it

die on her lips. Her stomach began to rumble as she followed him, and she hoped it was out of earshot. She watched the muscles of his back strain against his T-shirt as he lifted first one bag then the other into the bed of the truck. Each landed with a thud, and he turned to take her burden.

"I got it," she declined, using both hands to lift it.

Dalton's face scrunched up in disagreement, his brows thatching on his forehead, and she had the feeling that she'd been scolded without a word. He wriggled his fingers as he reached, taking it from her.

Instantly, the weight disappeared, and she lost her balance for a millisecond. In the next instant, the bag landed in the bed.

"Thank you for everything today, Dalton. That was above and beyond the call of duty," she said.

He waved her off. "I know a little about what you're going through. Glad to be the friendly hand," he replied, opening the driver's door. "I hate to mention it, but I see you're wearing yesterday's cutoffs. There's a couple thrift stores down the road from the urgent care. Keep going straight. First one's on the right. Other's on the left. In case you needed a pair on the cheap."

She smiled around the heat creeping up her neck and gave him a thumbs up. "Thanks!"

He lifted his hand and shook it sharply twice then dropped into the truck. The engine started smoothly, and she watched him buckle in before driving away.

Wondering if she'd stared too long after his taillights, she returned to chip away at her inheritance.

FOUR

SEVERAL DAYS LATER, with a mild headache, Analese finally took a break, easing into one of the rigid kitchen chairs. Her back ached; her arms ached; her torso ached. Even her hair hurt. She had reached the stage she had expected to find the place in when she arrived. The floors were clear and most of the surfaces had been cleared. Next would come the closets.

Since Dalton had helped a few days prior, she had found a tempo that helped her remain dispassionate about the items in her care, and she'd made a lot of headway. The bedroom, bathroom and kitchen had been scoured. It would need another clean before it was saleable, but at least she wasn't afraid to cook. And she was desperately tired of cleaning.

When she'd discovered her mother was living in a mobile home at a trailer park, she hadn't anticipated needing more than a week, but it was now Friday, and she could see there was at least another five days of work left.

How had her mother's life come to being obsessed with things and had so many that she couldn't even reach them? The house was stuffed with boxes and plastic bags full of things.

There had been a thought process behind each purchase, she could see. It was like strata of the Earth where she jumped on different fads and trends. One layer might be crafting items for wood engraving, the next, a set of cookbooks and measuring tools. So many items were in their original packaging, never opened. Then there were layers of leftover butter or whipped topping containers. Then a layer of mail or cards with nothing more than a signature inside. Straw baskets. Dried up pens and markers. Lanyards. Promo cups and water bottles, often cracked and unusable. Hairy lip balms, kernels of popcorn, and stray corn chips.

Even though the anger was beginning to subside, she couldn't help comparing the current state of affairs to how life had been growing up. Things were never perfectly organized or attractive. But there weren't piles upon piles of stuff. She saw so many things her mother had begged for in her thirties and forties. Dolls and toys that gave the impression she was still trying to obtain everything she had ever wanted but never received. Analese recognized that there was a mental illness or trauma there. And part of her felt guilty for not standing up for the woman. But her mother had made the environment so toxic, the only thing she could do was pull away.

Her parents' divorce had been ugly. Things had been brewing for more than a decade. But when the papers had finally been served and the dividing of property began, it was diabolical. The day she found the house locks changed had been the final straw.

"No," she told herself out loud. "No. That's over. She's dead. You need to let go of it."

Analese closed her eyes, laying her head in her hands. Upon hearing the news of her passing, her brother had told her she couldn't be hurt anymore. But he wasn't here sitting amongst the detritus of her greedy life. She surveyed the space. Only a few closets left and the spare room, and then she could wash her hands of it. Move on. Pretend she'd been hatched.

She inhaled deeply, utterly distracted by the scent of grilling meat. It smelled like hamburgers or steaks — she couldn't be sure which, except that she was in the middle of a trailer park. She moved to the window over the kitchen sink. No one was outside. Shifting down the hall, she peered out a window on the other side and spied white smoke rolling over the sloped ground leading to the next row of homes.

Gulping back the hunger that burbled up in her belly, she shoved the jealousy down and peered into the small fridge to see what she could muster to alleviate the hunger.

A knock on the door interrupted her.

Martin was on the stoop, his jeans still at half-mast like the last time.

"Hi, Martin," she greeted.

Without waiting for an invitation, he stepped inside, staring unabashedly around at her work. "Wow! It's nearly livable in here," he complimented.

She rested against the kitchen counter, nodding. "Yes. I'm not just playing tiddlywinks in here."

"Girl, I'm impressed." He stared openly at her, hands poised on his hips.

"Thanks," Analese replied.

"So, you're not from around here, and I know you and your mom didn't talk. So you probably don't know that we have a potluck every month. And you're the talk of the park," he explained.

She frowned. She wanted to be snarky, but she needed to be in this man's good graces. "Is that so?" she finally asked.

"You should come."

She looked behind her at the empty counters. "I don't have anything to bring," she offered.

"Nonsense. You're the dish they all want a taste of."

Her nose wrinkled. "That sounds…"

"Creepier than I planned," he finished, laughing. "Come on. I brought the golf cart. I saw that bandage you had, and Dalt told me about the stitches."

She sighed. She was starving, and this did explain the heavenly scent wafting through the area. "Can I clean up first?"

He narrowed his eyes. "Long as it don't take more

than a minute. We're all old folks round here. You ain't got nobody to impress. We're all jealous you've still got hair."

Analese cackled, clapping a hand over her mouth.

"I'll be fast like a bunny," she promised. The prospect of free food, despite who prepared it, was enticing. If nothing else, she could choke down a burger and pick at weird salads and side dishes. If she was lucky, there could be a cookie or a pie to finish it off.

She rushed to the bathroom, washed her arms, then darted to the bedroom to put on her secondhand jeans and a fresh T-shirt. She was running a brush through her hair, parting it on one side as she exited the bedroom.

"Let's go."

Martin nodded his approval and was already on the porch and halfway to the golf cart by the time she'd locked the front door.

"I'll ask Dalt to come by and look at the front door. Your mom slammed that thing like a trucker just getting her mail. Warped the hell out of it."

Her brows arched. "It would be nice for the front door to work when I sell," she mused.

"Damn straight," he agreed.

The cart whirred as he sped down the paved asphalt pathway that wove through the grounds. "Your mom was right proud of you when she wasn't cryin' about how you were going to hell."

Analese scoffed. "I was always intrigued at how she always knew what I was doing and where I was even though we hadn't spoken in twenty years. Downright creepy."

"Told us she used her DMV contact and some folks from a courthouse lookin' in on you."

Analese shook her head and rolled her eyes. "Shouldn't surprise me. She could get some pretty shady stuff done when it served her purpose."

"So you did know her," Martin ribbed.

Analese smiled but said nothing as he hooked a right toward the smell of a working grill.

FIVE

THE CART ROLLED TO A STOP after another moment, and Analese looked out over roughly three dozen white and gray heads milling from lawn chair to lawn chair in varying states of decay. He hopped out more nimbly than she expected and ambled toward the row of tables with mismatched vinyl clothes flapping in the gentle breeze. One was red checkered, another covered in grape vines, and one was covered in reindeer and Santas.

The food available looked like it went on for football fields.

At the end was a large steel grill. An elderly gentleman with an apron stood at the helm, a greasy spatula extended from his fist planted firmly on his hip. A wisp of hair on the top of his head waved at her as he stared down at the man on the ground below the grill.

Dalton was crouched on the ground, both arms stretched under the cart, and she realized he was installing a new gas tank. It had to be hot, she imagined, from the way he kept pulling a hand out and then reaching back in.

"I told you the flame was too high, Hank," Martin called. "It's not fair to Dalt to have to change it while it's hot."

"Dalton," Dalton called back, freeing his hands and wiping them on the grass on either side of him. "It's not Dalt."

Martin tipped his baseball cap in Dalton's direction. "Sorry."

Dalton nodded back at him before turning his eyes on her. "I'm not used to seeing you outside of your natural habitat. Almost didn't recognize you."

She chuckled, thinking how right he was. The first time he'd seen her, she'd been crying and covered in blood. The next time, she'd only just rolled out of bed. She must have looked like a homeless person.

"I see you're hard at work as always," she noted.

He smiled, making no excuses, then stood. "Light her up, Hank. You should be good to go now." Dalton shuffled toward a medium-sized pole barn about ten yards away, hands aloft to show off how dirty they were.

As though someone had put a quarter in him, Hank ratcheted into motion, lifting the grill lid.

Smoke billowed out around them, and Analese backed up to sputter.

Martin didn't even seem to notice. "Lookin' good. You think two minutes?"

Hank's thumb and index finger curled into a circle, and he fanned the other three fingers out behind it.

"If you'll stop distracting me," he groused.

Turning back to her, Martin waved at the smoke and toddled toward the buffet. "Now, here's the plates and forks. Napkins here." He pointed. "Get yourself a plate filled up, and I bet Hank'll have a burger for you in no time."

Noticing that everyone else was already indulging, she followed his instructions and circled back to the grill when she was done. She waited awkwardly for Hank to acknowledge her.

"You ready, missy?"

"Yes, sir," she answered. She had a bun ready to go, one half doused in mustard and ketchup, the other with cheese and lettuce. A slice of tomato was making a run for it across her plate but landed in a mound of bright yellow potato salad.

Hank pulled a cheese covered burger fresh off the grill and expertly shimmied it off the spatula onto her bun without making direct contact.

"You're a little young to be hanging round these parts," he noted.

Analese flipped the top bun and condiments onto her burger. "Yes, sir. I'm just cleaning out my mother's house," she replied, licking ketchup off her thumb. "Martin said I should come to the potluck. I hope that's okay."

Hank's eyes met hers in understanding as he nodded, then reached out to touch her forearm lightly. "I'm so sorry for your loss. That must make you Ana."

She nodded, uncomfortable at both his touch and the use of her short name.

"That's me. In the flesh," she answered. Reflexively, she started to ask if he knew her, but realized she didn't care. "Thanks so much for the burger. It smells divine." She lifted her plate a few inches. "I'm going to take advantage of this while it's fresh off the grill."

"Enjoy!" Hank called as she retreated.

Most all the tables were full, and she resigned herself to taking up the end of a table with only one other person seated. He was younger than the others, roughly her own age, she assumed. His shoulder-length hair was some shade of dark that was difficult to ascertain from the amount of oil in it. Whether it was intentional or a lack of cleanliness, she couldn't tell. But he looked harmless enough hunched over his plate and scooping up a spoonful of beans. Across the table from him was a full plate, fork lodged in a pile of coleslaw. However, the seat was unclaimed.

She waited till she was at the empty edge of the table across from him before she spoke. "Is it okay if I sit here?"

He looked up briefly, and she was intrigued by the storm-blue eyes that met hers.

"Sure. Knock yourself out," he welcomed.

His friendly tone was juxtaposed to the statement, but she felt like not accepting now would be an insult.

"Thanks," she answered, slipping onto the end of the picnic bench. It was an old, wooden park-style model that was all one piece, but it was sturdy, and she was glad to rest her plate on its surface.

The man at the other end returned to his victuals as though he was still alone.

Analese sighed relief as she spread her napkin over her lap and dug in. The first bite of the burger elicited a happy yelp, and she smiled as she chewed slowly, savoring each burst of salty meat, gooey cheese, and crunchy lettuce. She closed her eyes, ignoring the stares she felt from other tables. She knew that they would begin descending like gnats buzzing around an unguarded piece of food. She had better enjoy the moment of solitude while she could.

When the bench shifted under the weight of another person, she startled, nearly dropping her glorious burger. Beside her, Dalton folded himself into the bench. She wiped her mouth with her napkin furiously, then lifted a hand in greeting as she chewed.

He waved back picking up his fork.

"Van, this is Analese," Dalton introduced. He pointed across the table with his fork. "Analese, this is my best friend, Van."

The dark-headed man set down his utensils and swallowed, then smiled at her. "Hey."

"You'll have to forgive Van," Dalton explained. "He's a little shy."

"Hey, man," Van retorted, "It's not just me. She had every chance to introduce herself, and she said nothing either."

Analese nodded, noting the stubble coating Van's face. It made him look scruffy, perhaps, but also like he knew his way around many manly activities like chopping wood and running tractors.

"He's not wrong. It's rare to meet someone as shy as I am," she agreed.

Dalton rolled his eyes. "Scared of your own shadows." He switched out his fork for a cob of corn and bit into it, spraying juice across the table on his friend.

Van cursed, drawing back and scooting toward

the middle of the table. "Not safe eating with you."

"At least it's just corn and not dentures flying across the table," Dalton teased back quietly.

Analese fought not to laugh too loud. She poked at her food.

"Food's good," Dalton countered.

Van shrugged.

"Free food is free food," Analese added bravely.

Van tilted his head in her direction with a smirk and an arched brow. "Where did Dalton find you?"

"Mary's daughter," Dalton answered, wiping corn and butter from his cheeks.

"Oh." Van tucked himself around his plate again, scooting in Dalton's direction almost imperceptibly.

"I take it you knew her," she retorted.

Van chuckled.

"Van and I work together, but we've been buddies since grade school," Dalton explained. "Born and raised in this armpit of a town. And before you ask, Van is the brother in Boris Brothers."

"Oh, so you're famous!" she exclaimed.

Analese thought she had screamed something vulgar judging by the expression on Dalton's face.

54

Now *he* was folding in on himself around his food. It was like he'd smelled a fart! She glanced at Van for some hint at what she'd said to evoke such a reaction.

"Naw," Van replied, eyeing a forkful of beans. "Not famous. We don't do famous here."

She neutralized her expression as Van discreetly slashed his hand across his throat. She took a bite of her burger with a soft groan.

"There you go…giving it away again for free," Dalton scolded.

Analese shrugged. "Call it charity."

Van wrinkled his nose at her. "We don't do charity, either."

"Settle down, Van," Dalton chided. "We're good. Ana's here to clear out the trailer and sell it."

Van scraped the last bit of potato salad from his plate. "You're gonna be here a while," he stated.

She shook her head, preparing for another bite. "I'm making good headway. I'm hoping to set a date for a yard sale soon with Martin."

Van chewed up his bite and swallowed, still smacking his lips as he replied. "You could have that place painted up like the White House, and you still gotta find an old person who wants to buy anything. Ain't nobody movin' to Erin."

Momentarily discouraged, Analese chewed on her burger, the taste forgotten as his words impacted her.

"My mom did."

He scoffed, wiping his hands on a crumpled paper towel. "That don't make no sense to me either." He tossed his soiled napkin and empty cup onto his plate and looked to Dalton. "You nearly finished? One of them could expire before you play, and you know that's what they're all here for."

Without further ado, Van lifted himself off the table, and the bench shifted suddenly, now that it was unevenly weighted.

Dalton and Analese yelped, grabbing their plates and attempting to stand briefly.

"Chickens," Van mumbled with a grin as he walked toward the pole barn.

The table settled, and Analese switched sides. "Can't risk another trip to the urgent care. Insurance is out now."

"Hey, I heard yesterday that one of the thrift stores is looking for help if you wanted something temporary. It's not glamorous, but it'll keep you in jeans with two legs for a while if you're interested."

She chuckled. "I might have to be."

He stood, picking up his plate. "It's that first one past the urgent care."

"Thanks," Analese called back.

Six

AS SHE WATCHED HIM GO, she nibbled at her food. She liked the way he walked, discreetly tugging his jeans up when he thought no one was looking, combing stray locks of hair out of his eyes. She was measuring the distance between his hips and the ground when she realized that he was joining Van in front of the pole barn. Three bales of hay were arranged in front of the door, two stacked with one lone bale next to it.

Van was crouched beside a short, black box, twisting its dials. On top of the speaker was a geometric half dome ringed by a set of colored lights. It was a karaoke machine that looked like a roadhouse bar rescue. A microphone on a stand wrapped in duct tape wobbled in the breeze.

The last thing she expected to see was both of them strapping on acoustic guitars. Dalton straightened his over his hips, pulling a pic from the coin pocket of his jeans. He held it over his head, and the community started cheering.

Dalton braced one foot on the microphone base and leaned forward till his mouth nearly touched it.

"Thank you for coming out tonight," he greeted. His voice boomed across the onlookers, and they thrilled at the sound.

A few loud whistles answered him, and he cast his eyes at his guitar, pretending not to be amused as he plucked a string to tune it.

Van began pacing, strumming a few random chords.

"While we've still got time, Dalton!" one of the women called back.

"Alright," he agreed, waving a hand their direction before beginning to play an intricate melody at a medium pace, and Van joined in, strumming along.

Analese stopped eating, turning her attention to the duo as Dalton began to sing. His voice was neither high nor low, but something comfortable and natural sounding to a man his size and shape. His words were earnest, and while she had never heard the song before, she noticed a few of the patrons mouthing the words. Nearly all of them were tapping a toe or clapping to the beat.

She was so enthralled as he wove a spell over the group, that she barely noticed when a squat woman took a seat on the other side of the picnic bench until she felt its balance shift, and she looked up.

"You must be Ana," the woman said.

She sighed and smiled with a quick nod, hoping the stranger would get the hint. She wanted to watch Dalton and Van. They were an impressive duo.

"I'm Judy. Your mom's neighbor."

She tore her gaze from Dalton's mouth as he belted out a note and let out a sigh as she looked at the newcomer again.

"Nice to meet you," Analese replied.

"You been throwing out an awful lot of her stuff. She'd be so mad," Judy accused.

She nodded. "I believe it." She looked away to watch Dalton and Van.

"She wouldn't be very kind about you lusting after those boys either. Godless. Both of them," Judy grumbled, shaking her head.

Analese kept her mouth shut, folding her hands in her lap and listening as Dalton held a long, curvy note. It had been a long time since she'd heard a live band, but she was certain this was above par.

"How come you never came to visit your mother? You broke her heart, you know," Judy continued.

Releasing a long breath, Analese looked Judy square in the face, studying the lines and wrinkles. Her pudgy cheeks were speckled with age spots, and there was a thick, two-inch snow-white hair dangling from the corner of her jaw. It matched the shorter ones on the corners of her mouth. Her thinning hair was clipped back severely against the side of her head with two plastic barrettes. Her milky green eyes widened, as though she was afraid, when Analese leaned in to answer.

"Honestly, Judy, I valued my sanity too much."

Judy gasped, drawing back with a hand to her chest. "That's an awful thing to say."

"Oh," Analese gasped, mimicking the gesture. "I thought that's what we were doing. We've never met before today, but you're full of assumptions on things you know nothing about."

"Well, she was sure right about you," Judy growled.

Analese smiled prettily at her then turned bodily to face Van and Dalton. She felt the weight of the table shift. Moments later, she saw Judy's back as she made her way to the buffet. With an exaggerated motion, she snatched a baking dish from the table, bits of food flying as she stormed down the path to resident housing.

Returning to her burger, Analese hummed in delight at the mouthful of warm meat and the anonymity of listening to music without anyone interrupting.

Dalton's lyrics were laced with a sense of longing and loss that felt like a warm blanket on a lonely winter afternoon. They were beautiful in their simplicity but tugged at her heart, and she wondered what had inspired them.

Van was no slouch either, at one with the counter melody to Dalton's lead. She had no idea how he saw what he was doing with all his hair falling over his face as he played. Any shyness she had seen in him disappeared as he played.

Her table shifted again to her surprise, and she found Martin sitting down. He slid a small paper plate toward her. A piece of pie with a fork sticking straight up from the center stared back at her.

"You looked like you could use a piece," he muttered. He had a slice of his own, shoveling down half in his first bite.

"Thanks," she murmured.

Dalton's voice begged for her attention, and she turned to watch him, body pressed to the mic, eyes closed, and face strained as he belted out a clear, strong note. It was one of the purest things she'd ever seen.

"He shoulda gone to Hollywood," Martin noted.

She didn't disagree. While the flavor of the music was more country than her rock and roll tastes, she recognized the talent.

"Or at least Nashville," he added.

She sighed as the song ended and the crowd applauded earnestly. She joined them enthusiastically, clapping till her palms ached. She turned to Martin.

"Why didn't he?"

Martin shoved another large bite into his mouth instead of answering.

She sensed a story there. Maybe he didn't know. Or maybe he didn't want to tell.

Another song began, and she worked on polishing off her dinner before sampling the gifted dessert.

"Judy and your mom were like oil and water," Martin stated.

She set down her fork. "She seemed more like her twin."

Martin barked out a laugh so loud, it drew the attention of neighboring tables. He glanced at her from his plate and back. "That's good. But don't ever let her hear you say that."

They listened to the music for a while longer, until another woman approached, gathering plates before anyone could stop her. The dirty look she left with Analese, however, lingered.

She glanced at Martin. "What was that about?"

"Don't mind her. She hated your ma and everything associated with her. Called her trash. And a few other things." He snickered under his breath.

She smiled. It was curious how Martin had no trouble telling her all about the residents but clammed up when it came to the neighborhood handyman.

"How long have you been here, Martin?" she questioned.

He arched a brow. "Before I could live here, that's for sure. And I been living here for nigh on fifteen years next summer."

"You must know everything about everything."

He shook his head, turning to face Dalton and Van. "Darling, you get to my age you realize you don't know nothin' 'bout nothin'."

She giggled and matched his pose, facing the men singing across the park. They ended another song and rolled right into the next one. The tunes were unfamiliar but catchy, and she giggled as Van strummed his guitar dramatically then popped up like a jack in the box to sing backup.

They played for close to an hour to thunderous applause. Analese counted her good fortune that no one else bothered her while Martin was nearby.

She watched absently as Dalton put his guitar

away in a case that had been sitting nearby the whole while. Several of the residents swarmed him, and he smiled politely as he worked. She found herself hoping he would come her way to eat or chat. However, he simply strolled toward his truck, stowing his guitar in the back seat, two stragglers remaining by the time the door slammed shut.

Martin left to help Van roll the grill back in the barn, and Analese felt eyes on her from the remaining residents like vultures eyeing roadkill. She limped toward her mother's trailer before they could take a bite.

SEVEN

THE FOLLOWING AFTERNOON, while working through the stack of boxes in the corner of the bedroom, a rap sounded on the front door frame. Analese had propped the door open with the screen in place to keep out the big bugs.

"Ana?" the voice called.

She recognized Dalton immediately and grinned.

"I'm in the back!" she bellowed.

The screen door popped as it released, and she heard his footsteps as he entered.

Analese wiped her hands against her jeans as she met him.

"AC not working?" he asked when she joined him.

She shrugged. "As well as it always has. I opened a box this morning that smelled pretty strongly. Needed some air."

"Ah." He nodded adamantly. "You also need new

carpet. This stuff was shot when she got here, and…" he paused, his eyes darting to the open door. "You need new."

Analese frowned. "I've been trying to ignore it. I don't know how I'll afford it."

He arched a brow, puffing out his chest as he rested his hands on his sides. "Have I got the deal for you," he announced.

"Is that so?" She grinned openly at his stance, leaning against the kitchen counter.

He nodded. "How do you feel about wine?"

"As a rule, I think it makes a terrible stain, and nobody likes my taste in it."

Dalton chuckled. "As a color, silly. A friend of mine offered me some leftovers from a job he did in Nashville last week. But it's some kind of sculpted wine-colored thing. I've got it and the matching pad in the truck." He gestured with a thumb toward the street.

"It sounds horrible," she replied.

He laughed. "It sounds free and clean." He pointed to the matted beige acrylic pile beneath his feet.

"It sounds perfect," she answered, clapping.

"I thought so too. Help me carry it in?" he asked.

"Sure," she answered, straightening. "But where are we going to put it?"

She scanned the front room with some boxes she still had to sort through, the table and its four chairs, and a rickety bookshelf brandishing a handful of items.

"Well…I've been thinking about that on the drive over here. I thought if we could wrestle it in the living room, we could put it where the couch used to be, and maybe this weekend I could get Van to help install it."

Tears welled in her eyes without warning. "Oh, Dalton, that's so much work."

"I got nothing else to do."

She stared at his face for what felt like an eternity. Why did he care about her or this trailer? Why would he sacrifice his time to help her? There was nothing between them.

"But!" he added, crossing his arms sternly, "You gotta get this place ready to receive it,"

"What does that mean? Like rip out the carpet that's here?"

He shook his head. "No. That'll take like two minutes, and Van likes to destroy stuff."

She laughed. "Well, what then?"

"First, this place needs to be totally empty. I mean, everything's gotta come out. Secondly, have the trash bags and broom ready to go. And maybe you could beverage us while we work. Like — play nurse in case we need something."

"Why, Dalton, are you asking me to play nurse with you and your friend?" The moment the words left her lips, she regretted them.

Dalton, however, laughed. "That's good."

"How do you feel about tea?" she asked.

He nodded. "Perfect. Let's get that carpet inside."

She followed him outside, gasping when she saw the long tubular load in the back of his truck. "You really think I can carry half that?"

"We're about to find out," he replied, letting the gate down.

Wine colored fibers poofed out the end of the carpet, and Analese waved them away. Her first thought was how dark the interior would be followed by how it would be clean, and some of the smell might disappear.

She wrapped her arms around the bundle, her hands not meeting around the load. Dalton somehow took the lion's share of the weight, allowing her to set the pace as she struggled toward the front door. She climbed the stairs shakily, harrumphing when she dropped her end inside the doorway.

"Oh, that's okay," Dalton grunted, pushing her end inside another two feet. "I've got it." He tipped the carpet roll opposite himself. "Timber!"

It thudded against the living room wall. The pad was much lighter, and she managed to carry it all the way inside and rest it gently beside the other roll.

He dusted off his hands on his shirttails. "You have till 8 a.m. Saturday to get ready. See you then!"

True to his word, at 7:59 a.m. Saturday morning, she heard the distinct sound of a pickup out front. She leaned over the kitchen sink to watch, gaping as Dalton's white pickup backed all the way up to the door, the grip slipping over the wet grass before coming to a halt. The truck lurched to a stop, the engine dropping off a moment later.

She hurried to the door, throwing it open as the driver's side opened, and Van emerged, his hair damp around his shoulder. Dalton, dressed in his usual ensemble, a tight ponytail running down his neck, emerged from the passenger door.

"I'm impressed you let someone else drive your truck," she called.

"It's *my* truck," Van announced, slamming the door. "Technically."

"I have batter and eggs ready. I was about to pull bacon out of the oven," she greeted.

"Whoa! Did you win the lottery?" Dalton called.

She chuckled. "No, but there was a pastor who came by Thursday with a box of food from the church pantry."

Van grunted. "Church bacon," he echoed. "Think it'll taste holy?"

Dalton chuckled. "Just eat the pig, Van." He turned his gaze to Analese. "Fire up the grill for those hotcakes while we pull the roll out. We won't want to eat while we're pulling up the pad."

"Yeah, could be a whole family of something living

72

in there," Van agreed.

Analese nodded, rushing in to pull the tray of fried goodness out of the oven, humming at the sight of foam rolling over each bumpy strip. Within moments, she had eggs scrambling in one pan and pancakes coalescing in another. She glanced to the front door as the men skipped up the stairs. Without a sound, they lifted one end of the carpet roll on each of their shoulders and walked it outside. They returned for the pad.

She shook her head, flipping a cake and thinking they were both incredibly strong. She remembered the weight of the new carpet from the painkillers she required the following day, and they made it look like carrying a newspaper.

Van and Dalton made brief appearances in the doorway, setting a variety of tools in the room before joining her.

She set two plates on the counter as the last pancake was developing in the skillet.

"You got a future as a short order chef," Dalton complimented as he took a seat.

Van had already inhaled a mouthful of eggs. He

shoved half a strip of bacon in his mouth with one hand while he carved a chunk of cake with his fork.

"Good too," he agreed.

By the time she'd joined them at the table, Van's plate was veritably empty.

"You weren't hungry," she teased.

He gave a lopsided grin. "Life's short."

"Thanks for breakfast," Dalton added.

"It's the least I could do. Not only for free carpet, but all this labor, too. I'll be in your debt forever."

"We don't do debt around these parts," Van retorted. "You done yet?" He eyed Dalton, rising to set his plate in the kitchen sink. "You eating or makin' love to 'em?"

Dalton snorted, shoveling half a pancake into his mouth. His cheeks bulged like a chipmunk's as he chewed. He picked up his last slice of bacon, nibbling as he moved across the room. Van was already running a box knife around the edges of the carpet.

Analese scooped up her plate and Dalton's, tossing them in the sink as well.

"You might not want to be in the room for this,"

Dalton suggested.

She nodded, absconding to the bedroom and pulled the door almost shut.

"Aw man," she heard Van mutter. "You think there's critters living in this?"

Hiding in the doorway, Analese spied on the pair.

"We already found a nest of mice," Dalton replied, kneeling with his back to her to cut another strip in the flooring.

Van grumbled, dropping to his knees to work as well. "You're gonna owe me more than a case of beer for this."

The sound of box cutters against carpeting covered the sound of her closing the door.

She was down to half a dozen boxes of assorted junk, a mangled jewelry armoire, and the nightstand. The sound of carpet being yanked off the floor filtered through the closed door as she set the first box on the bed. It was full of pictures, and part of her wanted to sort through them. Mary had made off with most of the family pictures after the divorce, and for the first time since arriving, Analese was grateful for the find.

The next two boxes were filled with assorted vests and handbags that had been encased so long the vinyl had cracked and adhered itself to half the contents. It wasn't even worth donating!

"Shit!" Van's voice filled the trailer, and she heard tools hitting the ground. "What the hell?"

Analese cringed at the noise. They had warned her to close the door.

Determined to push through her tasks, she pulled open the bottom drawer of the nightstand, finding nightshirts and a few particularly disturbing negligees. She emptied the contents into the box full of melted purses then yanked open the top drawer.

Two long, clear bottles rolled to the front. At first, she assumed it was lotion, but it couldn't have been. The viscous clear liquid oozed from one side to the other with the motion. Next to it was a rubbery tube with a hard plastic cap on one end. It was blue and glittery, and she reached to inspect it. However, moments before her fingers made contact, she realized what it was and let out a shriek that hurt her throat, slamming the drawer shut.

She bolted from the room, barely noticing that

Dalton and Van were practically doing a jig stomping on a swarm of what she had to assume were roaches crawling out from beneath the padding. Analese didn't pause on her way out the door, flying down the stairs and pacing across the front yard.

She had nearly touched the thing in the drawer! Shaking her hands and squealing, Analese squeezed her eyes shut. "No, no, no. You did not just see that," she consoled herself.

"Ana?" Dalton's voice carried to her, and she looked over her shoulder to see both men racing behind her.

"You okay?" Dalton pressed.

"What the hell did your mom do in there? Breed those damn things?" Van rambled.

She waved a hand at them both. "I found something… unexpected in her nightstand."

"She have a gun in there? I got a guy who can handle that," Van offered.

"No." The word came out with a few tears attached. "But I am never opening that drawer again. In fact, I'm bringing the whole nightstand outside now, and we can throw it out with the garbage."

Van's face was wrinkled in confusion.

Analese saw the moment that understanding dawned on Dalton.

"Is it a heavy nightstand?" he asked.

"I'll get it," Analese insisted. "It shocked me...and I needed some air."

"Don't be stupid," Dalton retorted. "I'll get it. Wait here. I promise not to open the drawers."

"Maybe we can burn it," she advised.

"Marshmallows!" Van suggested. "Can't let a good fire go to waste."

"No!" Analese denied. "No! I don't want to put anything in my mouth that's been near what's in that drawer."

"She got a Bob in there or something?" Van replied with a chuckle.

"What's a Bob?" Analese asked, then wondered if he knew the thing's name.

"Battery operated boyfriend," Van supplied.

Her chin dropped open, and she stared in disbelief.

"Oh, hell. That ain't nothing. It's an old folk's

home. I bet they all got 'em, the way the mailman keeps delivering those brown boxes," Van explained.

Analese groaned, folding herself in half till her head was on her knees. "Make him stop talking!"

"Knock it off, Van," Dalton scolded.

"I don't know what the big deal is. Everyone does it," Van complained. "It's natural!"

Dalton stared at him, face tight. "She's a lady, man."

The two exchanged looks for a long minute, silent.

Dalton broke the battle of wills first, turning his eyes to Analese. "Stay here. I'll go take the thing out."

"I need some roach spray," Van grumbled, stalking toward the truck. "Those things are not getting inside this truck."

Analese lifted a thumb in his direction, still doubled over and taking slow, deep breaths. She listened to the sound of the truck doors opening and then closing and footsteps fell between her and the mobile home.

"She was human too even if she acted like Satan," Van soothed. "Don't get too bent out of shape."

Unable to form words, Analese lifted her head slowly, running her hands over her hair to tame the ones that had slipped from her ponytail. She took one more deep breath, blinked, and faced Van as Dalton appeared in the doorway with the two-drawer stand in his arms.

"So how bad is the carpet?" she asked.

Van wagged the can of bug spray at her. "This oughtta help. But we gotta let it do it's magic before we go back in there.

Dalton clapped his hands together after tossing the furniture on top of the carpet refuse in the bed of the pickup.

"What do you say we spray, take this to the dump, and then come back and finish," Dalton suggested.

"Liquor store after the dump," Van interjected. "I'm too sober for this."

Dalton chuckled. "Sure." He turned to Analese. "You wanna come with? Take your mind off?"

She didn't hesitate in nodding. "Lemme get my purse and wash my hands."

"Why? Did you touch it?" Van teased, following her up the stairs.

Analese growled at him, swatting at his forearm.

80

EIGHT

BY THE TIME THE SUN WAS SETTING, Analese was seated around the burn pit at the back of Van's cabin. The carpet was installed, and the three of them were taking a well-deserved rest in a trio of rusted folding chairs. Her mother's nightstand was ablaze at the center of the circle, and she watched as flames licked the corners of the top. The veneer curled away as the particle board beneath writhed and blackened.

Van tossed an empty beer bottle at the fire, cheering when it smashed against the burning stand. "He shoots; he scores!"

Dalton passed him another from the cooler and extended one toward Analese. "Still nursing that one?"

"Yes, thanks."

"Drink up, girl!" Van encouraged. "The wicked

witch is dead. She ain't gonna bitch at you no more about it."

"So you did know her," she teased.

"You ain't even really drinking with those wine coolers." Van tossed his bottle cap into the fire.

Analese looked around as the last vestiges of the sun disappeared, leaving them in shadows. A crescent moon watched them overhead, and the stars began to come into view.

They were on acres of land. The dump they'd mentioned was a gully behind a dilapidated barn on the west side of his property. It was filled with fence posts, rusted pieces of roofing, and too many things to name. She supposed things were done differently in Erin than in South Bend.

"This is quite a property, Van," she noted. "Thanks for letting us burn the furniture and dump the carpet."

He grinned. "I like my space. Gotta have a place to unwind and burn shit."

"And drink," Dalton added.

They clinked bottles, Dalton shifting in his lawn chair before resting his empty bottle on the ground next to it.

"The new carpet looks great, guys," she complimented. "I don't know how to thank you."

She swore there was a wicked glint in Van's eye as he replied. "I'm sure we can think of something." He followed it with a long pull on his beer.

They were quiet for a moment, watching the fire as it curled the nightstand's top. One leg gave out, and it tipped to one side.

"So what do people do for fun around here outside of drink and burn stuff?" she questioned.

"Watch paint dry," Dalton answered quickly.

"And bumpers rust," Van added.

"And grass grow," Dalton finished. The pair shared a grin. "I don't know. There's a movie theater about twenty miles out. I dunno — we eat and shoot cans and stuff."

"And we play music," Van reminded.

"Yeah!" Analese replied. "That was amazing at the barbecue the other day. How long have you guys been playing together?"

Dalton shrugged. "I don't know if I can remember that far back. Kinda forever. My dad gave me an acoustic guitar for my ninth birthday that he found in a pawn shop in Nashville. And then Van made it some kind of competition, and here we are today, still trying to outdo each other."

She chuckled at the description, watching as Van finished his beer.

"Competition my ass," Van complained. "He's always been like a prodigy. Picked it up right away and started writing music in high school. That's how he got all the girls."

"I was not a playboy," Dalton refuted.

Van's gaze at his friend was accusatory, and Analese leaned in to hear him. "That's how you got Julie."

"Shows you how dumb I was," Dalton grumbled. He reached for a long piece of metal and poked at the fire. It tumbled under his ministrations, and the top drawer glowed with eerie white flames.

"Who's Julie?" Analese questioned. The way they were looking at each other, she was almost afraid to hear the answer. She was certain there was a story here.

Neither of them answered for a minute, and she resigned herself to not getting an answer.

"My ex," Dalton supplied. "She loved my music. Took me to Nashville once to record a demo."

"That's exciting," Analese complimented. She started to say more, but then stopped herself. Somehow the mention of his ex and his music didn't sound like a story that would end well. She wanted to hear about the demo. Wanted to know if they'd been married and for how long. But she tamped it down.

"Got any family back home?" Van asked.

She nodded. "Dad's still around. He and my brother live in the country outside of South Bend, but we don't see each other often. Mainly on long holiday weekends and the like. I have a sister-in-law, and two nieces."

"That's almost as much as this one," Van remarked, pointing at his friend. "One sister, one brother, five nephews, and me. And his parents."

Dalton glanced in the other man's direction. "I forgot how chatty you get when you drink," he commented.

Analese swallowed the last of her wine cooler. "Well, as satisfying as it is to watch this burn, maybe I should get one of you to give me a ride back before we're all three sheets to the wind."

"You can't leave," Van complained. "You only had one cooler, and we haven't had any shots!"

She chuckled. "You can drink the leftovers when no one's looking. It won't kill you."

Van waved his middle finger at her.

"Come on, Heathen. I'll take you back," Dalton offered, holding out his hand to Van for the keys.

The other man deposited them in his hand without flair. "Beer me," he ordered.

"Are you gonna be passed out by the time I get back?" Dalton questioned as he passed the requisite item to his friend.

"Neh, man. I'm only one sheet to the wind." He popped the cap and tossed it into the fire.

Dalton detoured by the stack of firewood nearby and threw on two logs the size of her thigh. Sparks licked the night air. He hooked a finger in her direction, and she followed him, waving back at Van with another call of thanks.

The truck revved to life under his gentle touch, and Analese buckled herself in. It had been strange riding in the back seat when they dumped the carpeting and deposited the foul nightstand in the fire ring. She was glad to be back up front where she felt less like a child.

"The work you've done in that place is amazing," Dalton complimented once they were on the road.

"Thank you, but as you know, I haven't done it alone. This stranger I met at the park came and helped me a lot. He's like a superhero in broad daylight. I should introduce you." She giggled at her own joke, smiling into the wooded distance.

"He sounds great. Unreal and like a total bore to be around, though. Tell him I'm single."

"Back off," she warned. "I'm single too, and I think he's straight!" The moment the words left her lips, she regretted them. This was the second time this week she'd slipped in an unintentional innuendo. What was it about this man that made her filter malfunction? "Wow — that was not where I'd planned to go with that."

"I'll blame it on the wine coolers," Dalton forgave. "Cooler. Boy, you're a cheap date."

The words gave her pause, even in her fuzzier-than-usual state. He'd had a beer too, and the conversation was friendly enough. Forcing her hackles down, she chuckled.

"My dad used to tell me that all the time."

Even in the dark, she saw his curious glance. The green glow of the stereo highlighted the arch of his brow. "You were raised by *two* monsters?"

Realizing how it could have sounded, she shook her head. "No. Nothing like that. It was a fond memory," she promised. "I sort of took pride in that as I grew up. Being a cheap date meant that I was easy to be with. Not a big commitment."

Silence stretched between them for a mile. "Parents are weird," he noted.

She smirked. "You ever had kids?"

"Nope. The missus left before we had to go through that," he replied.

His answer dissuaded her of the notion that maybe she should stop talking under the influence. This particular knife cut both ways, and maybe she could get answers to some of the burning questions she had about his personal life.

"So — you and Van. Born and raised here?"

"Yep…and grew up is more like it for Van. His

parents weren't around much. My parents thought they had an extra son."

She chuckled at the notion.

"But he's a good guy," Dalton defended. "Good heart. And I think all of us could use some of his ability to relax and let life roll off him like water off a duck's back."

"I could see that," she replied. "I've never seen anyone look that satisfied with an empty can of bug spray clutched in one hand."

His grin shone in the dash lights. "He does have an unhealthy delight for killing things. Critters, I mean. Not people. He only looks like an axe murderer."

Analese shook her head. "I've barely known you a couple weeks, and we're back to axe murderers. Is there something I should know about this town?"

He shook his head vehemently. "Nope. Nothing to see here. Move along."

She sighed as the laughter dissipated. "I'm gonna miss you when I go back to South Bend, Dalton. There's nobody like you up there. Or Van. Would both of you consider moving? I have a lot of domestic needs out that way with only my almost seventy-year-old dad and my over-forty brother, who has his own family to deal with."

He chuckled. "Neh, I don't think either of us would ever leave — not even with a glorious offer like all the home repairs we can stomach on the table."

"Oh, it's okay to admit it. You'll both be glad to see the back side of me when I go. I've been nothing but trouble." She fought back a frown, the words hitting closer to home than she'd expected. She was a burden to her family there, she was a burden to these fledgling friends here.

"It looks like you're about finished, actually. When are you going back?"

"I have a meeting with Martin tomorrow. We're going to talk about next steps. I've been applying for jobs while I'm between showers, but no bites yet."

"That's pretty quick. Looks like we got that carpet installed just in time. Garbage pickup is tomorrow too," he reminded.

She nodded, suddenly sad at the thought of leaving this sleepy little town full of chiggers and bad memories. She had grown accustomed to Dalton randomly showing up and making her mess of a life feel like everything was going to be okay.

"What time is your meeting with Martin?"

"Ten o'clock."

The road rumbled beneath them, and Analese's eyes followed the stars. She had thought South Bend had stars, but it was nothing like this place. There were twenty for every one she was used to seeing.

"We barely have a McDonalds, but we got all the stars you could ever want," Dalton observed.

"Well, that's something." She shifted her hands in her lap, picking at the dirt under her fingernails as they passed a random streetlight near an intersection.

"Hey, I'm curious," he asked after a beat. "What made your mother move here?"

Analese shrugged. "I don't know. I haven't talked to her in years. I'm sure she had a friend at a church somewhere who she told her sob story, and they had friends or relatives to foist her off on down here. I can't believe she wouldn't have told you. She loved to tell people things they never asked." She paused. "Or try to sell me off."

He cleared his throat.

"She didn't?" Analese gasped, then covered her face with her hands. "Oh, no. I am so sorry."

At this, Dalton chuckled. "Well, it was the only nice thing she ever talked about really. Glowing reviews one minute; heathen stories the next."

She heaved a sigh. "Well, I shouldn't be surprised. She worked at a licensing office years ago, and she tried to sell me off to so many people."

"How did you not kill her?" he asked.

"The grace of God," she replied. "I'd be getting out about now if I had…presuming any judge would've convicted me." She would've been convicted, she knew. It would have been premeditated – perfect – passionate. "She could be deceptively charming when you first met her. But her true colors didn't take long to come out."

"Van spotted her on the first try. Tried pawning you off on him, too. How he needed a good woman in his life," Dalton confessed.

Analese buried her head in her knees. "I can never look at him again," she groaned.

He laughed, patting the steering wheel as he tried

to stop. "Van's good people. He would never hold it against you."

"Still," she mumbled.

"Oh, come on. She's dead. She can't hurt you anymore. And eventually I bet you'll forget most of it."

"I could hope so."

He was right, of course. The finality of it all hadn't quite hit home yet, and for the first time, her heart relaxed. There would be no more incidents to add to her list of grievances. It was over, and maybe she could burn it like she had the nightstand and put it in her past.

Dalton turned the truck expertly into the community's drive and navigated to her temporary abode. He wiped tears from his cheeks as he shifted the vehicle into park.

"I haven't laughed like that in...I actually don't remember."

Reaching for the door handle, she offered him a wry smile. "I'm glad my pain has amused you. At least it was good for something."

The door groaned out a metal creak as she opened it, and Analese slipped to the ground then twisted to face him. "Thank you for everything today. You have a nice laugh. You should do it more often."

Dalton flashed a thousand-watt smile at her. "You're gonna make me blush."

She snickered, stepping back to close the door. "Aren't you lucky it's dark. Good night!" She shut the door and hurried to the trailer. The engine idled behind her until she turned the key in the lock. The moment she opened the door, the truck shifted gears and rolled away. She waved over her shoulder before heading inside.

The smell of roach spray had dissipated, but it lingered at the edge of her senses. Or maybe it was dye from the new carpet. But either scent was preferable to the odor that she hadn't been able to clean away in the last two weeks. The deep wine color was striking in the room, and tears threatened to spill down her cheeks at the improvement.

For the horror show her life had been, losing her job, having to clean up after her dead parent, and reliving the nightmares of her youth, somehow, she'd managed to find a handful of kind people in a town smaller than the company that had cut her from their payroll. The new carpet was stellar, but better sleep would be the result of knowing that the colony of insects were no longer festering under the acrylic pile.

The place was nearly ready. All she had to do was load a few boxes in the car, talk to Martin, and she might be able to get back to South Bend. Although, she wondered why she was anxious to get home. She hadn't heard a word from a single company where she had applied, and her first unemployment check hadn't cleared. None of her remaining family had called even once to check on her.

She was counting on Martin's assistance to sell, and if it hadn't been for Dalton and Van, and even Martin, she would never have gotten through this ordeal.

Between the work and the alcohol, Analese passed into a dreamless sleep in no time, fully clothed.

NINE

ANALESE HAD ALWAYS BEEN an early riser, but she cursed her own internal clock for continuing to wake her up shortly after 6 a.m. each day. She showered off the previous day's toil, dressed in a fresh pair of shorts and a simple, navy V-necked shirt.

She loaded the trunk of her car with the remaining boxes to keep or pawn. She hadn't decided yet if she would be better off pawning her goods in town or back at home, and she tucked the question into the back of her mind to ask Martin at their meeting.

She arrived at his office twenty minutes early, hoping he wouldn't mind. After she'd loaded the car and eaten breakfast, the boredom was overwhelming. She'd set the sheets to wash and trekked across the wooded lot for something to do.

A tiny, brass bell tinkled overhead as she pushed

the door to the front office open. The entire room was paneled. A random deer was printed on the fake oak veneer boards every few feet. She would have laughed if she thought she was alone, but the last thing she wanted to do was offend Martin. His office doubled as a general store, and three short shelves were stocked with chips, toilet paper, dish soap, and tiny tubes of ointments and rolls of antacids.

He was slumped at the counter near the register when she walked in, but he managed a meager wave as she approached.

"Morning, Martin," she greeted. "I hope you don't mind I showed up early."

He grumbled. "'S fine. Figured you'd wanna sleep in."

"I wish I could, but I've always been an early riser," she cited. She squinted at his posture. He was usually relaxed, hands clasped over the widest part of his belly as he leaned against the wall. There was even a worn spot in the paneling where his head usually rested. Today, he looked a little sweaty and more than a little strained.

"Everything okay?" she pressed.

"Oh, old age. Indigestion, I think." His voice was low and more gravelly than normal.

She frowned. "Spicy dinner?"

He chuckled and shook his head making a visible effort to appear relaxed on his bar stool. The exertion was fruitless however, Analese thinking he looked even less relaxed than before.

"Not on this no flavor diet doc's put me on. No salt. No red meat. Nothing fried. No sugar. It's enough to make a man wanna give up."

She nodded at the assessment. "That sounds awful. You feeling up to the meeting? I can come back."

He lifted himself from the stool and shuffled to the edge of the counter. "Come on. We'll go to the office so we can both sit," he grunted.

Analese had never seen him move so slowly.

"Are you sure you're alright? I don't mind."

"I said I'm fine, dammit," he groused. He waved a weak hand toward the back room.

Once seated on opposite sides of a broad, metal desk, his face began to relax. A manilla folder was open on his desk, and the upside-down forms were familiar. It was the loan paperwork on her mother's property. Documents that continued to swim before her vision when she tried to read them.

"So to be clear how this works, your mother owns the mobile home, but the land it's parked on belongs to the facility. Owners can use the land like it was theirs with a few restrictions. Lawn ornaments, a shed or carport if they want, but they are not allowed to build any additional livable structures. This is a mobile home park only."

He had given her the speech once before by phone, but now that she had spent some time in the area, his words carried more meaning.

"Yes, I recall you explained that," she confirmed. "I think it's actually ready for inspection to be sold. There's new carpet, and I've emptied out everything but the bed and the kitchen table and chairs like you asked."

"Good. Good."

For a moment, Analese wondered if he was a little drunk as he slurred the second "good." She waited for him to speak again, studying his elbows braced against the desktop.

He cleared his throat. "I've been thinking that because of all the work you've done, and the position you're in, I might consider…" he trailed off. He turned his eyes to meet hers, mouth partially open.

Analese wondered why he wasn't finishing his statement. One of his eyes blinked at her, the other shut. And then, like out of a horror movie, she noticed the closed eye looked like it was sliding down his face incrementally. She wondered if she was seeing things, but then she noticed one corner of his mouth slipping the same direction.

"Martin?" she gasped, jumping from her seat. She leaned over the desk, touching his hand. "Martin? Are you okay?"

He grunted.

When one half of someone's face began drooping, it could only mean one thing: he was having a stroke! If TV had trained her for anything, it was to spot a stroke or a heart attack. Analese grabbed the heavy black melamine receiver of his phone and cursed the rotary dial as she waited for the 9 to roll back into place so she could follow with two ones.

"911. What is your emergency?" the calm,

feminine operator requested.

"Hi, I think my friend is having a stroke. One side of his face drooped, and he's not answering me," she gushed, eyes blurry with unshed tears.

"Okay, ma'am. Remain calm. Is your friend breathing?"

Analese shoved her knuckles under his nose, feeling his breath hot against them. "Yes. Yes, he's breathing."

"Your friend needs medical attention. Can you give me your address?"

She panicked for a moment, but then grabbed an envelope from his desktop, reading off the information.

A near-silent hiss escaped the operator. "Ma'am, do you have a way to drive him to the nearest hospital?"

"I…" she panicked. "I have a car. But I can't lift him."

"Is there anyone nearby that can help you get him to a car?"

"No." Her voice cracked. "I…"

"Stay on the line, ma'am. I'm reaching out to

dispatch now."

Martin grunted as the operator put her on hold.

"Hang on, Martin." She squeezed one of his hands.

The still functional side of his face snarled, and he tried to say something. His good eye glanced across his desktop frantically. Following his gaze, she spied his cell phone.

"Who should I call?" she asked, gripping the phone receiver with her shoulder and grabbing the cell.

"Dal..." was all he could manage.

Remain calm, she told herself. His phone opened without a password, and she croaked a sigh of relief at his lack of security. Dalton's contact was easy to find, and she dialed it quickly and pressed it to the other ear.

Three rings passed before he answered. "Hey, Martin. Wha—"

"It's Analese."

"Ana?"

Her words came tumbling out. "Martin's having a stroke. I have 911 on the other line. I need help."

"Ma'am," the emergency operator interrupted. "Is he still conscious?"

"Yes," Analese gasped. "He's in his chair. We're in his office behind the counter."

"I'll be right there," Dalton promised.

A fat tear escaped over her eyelid, rolling down her cheek into the cell phone as the call disconnected. Her fingers relaxed long enough for the cell to crash against the desktop.

"Ma'am, what was that noise?"

"I'm sorry," she sniffed. "I dropped his cell phone. I've called someone to come help. He's on his way."

"Good. If your friend is having a stroke, we need to get him help in under three hours," she explained. "The ambulance is an hour away, and the nearest hospital is in Nashville."

"So you're telling me it's an hour to get him and two hours back? He'll never make it."

"The paramedics will begin treatment on site. But the sooner you can get him to the hospital, the better chance he'll have."

She repeated the words in her head. What chance? To live? To survive? And how had this responsibility fallen on her?

"Should we take him ourselves?" Analese offered.

"If possible, yes," the operator replied. "Stay on the line with me till the other person arrives. Is he still conscious?"

"Yes," Analese whispered, afraid to speak.

"Ma'am, can you tell me your name and the patient's name? Does he have a license?"

Focused on the task at hand, Analese found his wallet in his front shirt pocket. He tried to nod, but his body wasn't cooperating, and she squeaked as she caught him before he could tip out of the chair to the floor.

"It's okay, Martin. Stay still. Dalton's coming."

The older man sighed heavily, closing his eyes.

She rattled off the details from his ID and insurance cards to the emergency worker, and the operator put her on hold again to notify the hospital of their pending arrival. She tucked his cards back into place, clutching onto the worn, leather accessory still warm from his body and bit both her lips between her teeth.

Hold it together, Analese.

She wasn't sure why she was so near to losing her cool and sobbing over a man she barely knew who had been particularly rude to her for the first dozen calls they'd exchanged. This wouldn't happen in South Bend. In less than fifteen minutes, lights would be flashing outside the building, and at least two capable paramedics would enter, find them, and begin taking care of him, and she could probably go back home, leaving it in their hands.

Lost in a spiraling thought pattern, the tinkling of the bell over the front door brought her back to the moment. She swiveled to face the entrance.

"Ana? You back there?" Dalton called.

"Yes!" she yelled. Ana scrambled toward the front door, stretching the phone cord as she did so. "He's conscious and in his chair."

Dalton pushed past her, rushing to Martin's side. He kneeled next to the older man, pressing the back of his hand to Martin's forehead and patting his cheek.

"Martin, can you walk a little if I get you up?"

His question was calm but firm, holding the other man's gaze with his own.

Martin's head bobbled again, Dalton's hand steadying him.

"The ambulance is an hour away," Analese informed him.

"He can't wait that long. Hang up with the operator and help me get him to the truck," he instructed.

The operator's voice was tinny out of the receiver. "Ma'am, has help arrived?"

Analese turned back to the phone, answering rapidly. "Yes. Yes. We're going to get him to the truck, and I have to help."

"Good. I've informed the hospital that you're on the way."

Once the details were exchanged, Analese dropped the receiver into the cradle and moved to Martin's other side.

Dalton met her eyes. "Get your shoulder in his armpit," he instructed. "On the count of three, I'm going to lift him up, and you do the same. I think we can get him to the car."

She gulped but nodded, shifting into position. At the prescribed moment, she stood, shocked that between the two of them, they had him on his feet.

Martin's body was limp against Dalton, but the handyman gathered Martin to his side with one strong arm around his waist and clasping the hand draped over his shoulder. In no time, they were moving toward the doorway.

"I've got his wallet and IDs," she grunted as Martin's weight shifted between them.

Dalton hoisted the other man tighter against himself and kept moving.

"Good. I'll call Van to lock up once we're on the road."

They struggled lifting him into the back seat, but once he was in, the doors were closed, and Dalton sprinted to the driver's seat.

"Put on your belt and hang on," he warned.

Analese barely had the buckle clipped before he peeled away from the drive, gravel flying against the body of the truck. She cringed at the clattering bits as he swerved onto the main road. She gave him all the information from the operator about which hospital was ready to receive him, as he drove. She suddenly thought this must be what it felt like to be in the Indy 500.

Somehow, Dalton's focused expression was soothing, and as miles evaporated beneath his tires, she felt her breathing calm. She listened as he dialed Van on speakerphone and told him what was happening. Like Dalton, Van asked no questions and immediately stepped up to assist. The call was short, only the bare minimum of details exchanged.

The ride was too quiet, and Analase wondered what she'd pulled Dalton from mid-morning. He was dressed in his usual plaid shirt, T-shirt, and jeans. A brush of dirt stretched from his palm to his elbow, and a glob of spiderwebs clung to his knee.

"I'm sorry I called you," she apologized. "I didn't know who else..."

"I'm glad you did," he interrupted, eyes glued to the road as he wove around slower cars. "Martin's like family."

They were quiet the rest of the way to the hospital. Analese kept an eye on their passenger, squeezing his hand occasionally. She had never spent a longer drive in her life, praying for Martin to make it to the hospital and worrying that they'd get pulled over.

The only thing she didn't worry about was her safety as Dalton blazed a path to the hospital, cutting their time by at least thirty minutes.

Three hospital personnel were waiting for them at the emergency room with a wheelchair. The next minutes were a flurry of opening doors and answering questions while Martin was shifted into the chair by far more competent individuals.

"Stay with him," Dalton ordered as she reached to close the doors.

"I will," she promised. She slammed the passenger door shut, and the tires rolled forward with a squeal. She jumped, then raced after Martin.

Analese felt incredibly underprepared to deal with the situation.

"I'm just a tenant. We were talking, and he started...melting on one side," she rushed. She pressed his license and insurance card to a staff member with a clipboard before being ushered into a waiting room while nurses and doctors barked in code at each other while wheeling him away.

She was still staring after him when Dalton skidded to a stop in front of her.

"Where is he?" he snapped.

Analese pointed toward a set of double doors he'd passed through minutes ago. "They just took him back." She held up a clipboard and a pen. "I'm supposed to fill this out, but I can barely remember his last name."

With a sigh, he took the paperwork from her and dropped gently into the seat beside her.

"I can fill out most of this. You have his wallet?"

She nodded. "Yes, but I gave it to the registration lady. She's going to bring it back."

Dalton focused on the paperwork, and Analese watched helplessly. His handwriting was precise and unexpectedly neat for a man. She couldn't believe she was analyzing his printing skills when Martin was off in an unseen part of the hospital, probably having his clothes cut off like her jeans in the urgent care facility.

At that thought, she let the tears rush over her cheeks, trying to remain silent but for a sniffle and a low exhale.

Dalton stopped writing and rested his hand on her shoulder.

"Hey, it'll be alright. He's in good hands. It was a miracle that you were with him when it happened and reacted so fast."

She shook her head. "This is a nightmare." His fingers were warm against her shoulder, and the comfort simply encouraged her to cry more. "I'm sorry. I'll get it together. Don't let me distract you."

He passed her a box of tissues from a nearby chair and returned to the paperwork.

The registrar returned with Martin's cards, and Analese slipped them into his wallet gently while Dalton took over the check-in process. He certainly knew Martin better than she did, including the name of his doctor and even multiple medical conditions. He followed the registrar to her desk, and Analese took the opportunity to get a hold on her tears.

She realized in her haste, she had taken off without so much as her purse. She had no lip balm, no breath mints, no wallet. Her only respite was the cell phone tucked in her back pocket. She pulled it out, checking the time and then scanning the room till her eyes landed on the back of Dalton's head.

His hair was shiny, and his short ponytail had

flipped at the ends. It looked soft, and she imagined touching it. Her eyes spanned his broad shoulders and traced the lines in his plaid patterned shirt.

She wasn't sure how long it had been before Dalton returned, resuming the seat on her left.

"He's checked in," he announced. "I've got to call his sister." He freed his cell from his pocket and started searching his contact list. He glanced in her direction. "You okay?"

She nodded, offering a weak smile and dabbing at her eyes with the tissue clutched in her fingers. "I'm good. It all happened so fast. We sat down to talk and then..." Her mind replayed the event in slow motion for her. "I've never seen anything like it."

"I hope you never do again," Dalton comforted, patting her forearm. He shifted in the seat, stretching his long legs out ahead of him and crossing them at the ankles as he pressed the phone to his ear. He spoke softly. His charm was undeniable as he eased into the reason for his call. She wondered if he realized he was nodding during the conversation.

The call was blessedly short, and he slipped the

112

phone away. "Well, she's working on flights," he explained. "She's about ten years younger than Martin, but less healthy. I told her that we'd stay here with Martin until she can get here. I hope that's okay with you."

"Of course," Analese replied. Her brain sucked her down into another pitfall, however, and she squinted at the floor. "Um, except…well," she stuttered. "In all the chaos, I sort of…have nothing but my phone and the clothes on my back."

"Mmm," he hummed. "We can get through that. I'm not destitute."

"I am," she retorted. It was supposed to be funny, but it sounded sad amidst the beeping and pandemonium swirling around them. "Are they even going to tell us what's going on? We're not family."

"I'm his emergency contact in proxy for his sister. She's in Charlotte. We might be here for a couple days." He searched her face. "Are you okay with that? 'Cause I could call Van and see if he…"

"No, don't. I'll be fine. I'm unemployed and have no appointments." She wanted to mention that she also had no underwear, but she kept that part to herself.

"Thanks," he murmured.

About an hour later, a doctor approached, calling for Martin's family. They sprang to their feet, Dalton tugging his jeans up as he did.

The doctor was a short woman with a tight salt and pepper braid running down her back. "The good news is, Martin's going to be okay. You got him here in time."

Analese sighed relief.

"What's the bad news?" Dalton asked.

"He hasn't regained consciousness yet. He's stable and resting. We won't know much more until he wakes up. But we're expecting the best positive outcome. Your quick reaction time made all the difference."

"That's all her," Dalton praised. "Called 911 right away."

The doctor nodded at her. "We're going to keep monitoring him."

"Can we see him?" Dalton questioned.

"We've got him in ICU. Only one at a time," she cautioned. "There's a waiting room on that floor, so you won't be far from him. He's being taken there now. We're running some bloodwork and should have some answers soon." She gestured to a nearby nurse. "When Mr. Russell is settled in his room, would you please give this couple the information?"

Dalton thanked her profusely, and Analese found herself bobbing along with his intent. The next hour was a whirlwind of questions and getting lost in the halls before finding their way to ICU. The nurse stationed nearest Martin updated them on his condition as well as the location of the waiting room and the visiting hours which would be ending in roughly two hours.

She caught a glimpse of him propped in an uncomfortable looking bed, a series of tubes and wires connecting his body to a variety of machines like something out of a sci-fi movie. Dalton went straight in, pulling up a chair next to the bedside.

"The waiting room for ICU is down the hall on the left," a nurse noted.

Realizing the instructions had been for her, she nodded curtly and scurried in the direction indicated.

TEN

STARTLED BY A GENTLE NUDGE to the bottom of her foot, Analese popped up from her side to a sitting position. She blinked rapidly, the day's events coming back in a flood. She looked up to find Dalton staring down at her.

"How is he?" she questioned.

"No change," he replied. "But visiting hours are over, and they're kicking us out."

She frowned.

"I'm sorry I didn't come back to get you," he apologized.

Stretching, she shook her head awkwardly and launched to her feet.

"I won't accept apologies from you about this," she retorted. She straightened her shirt, smoothing out the sleeves and then wondering how much of her hair was standing on end after falling asleep on the vinyl loveseat.

"And the news gets worse," he added, leading her down the hall. "There's a convention in town. The closest room I could find is about twenty minutes south. And they only had one room. But I think it's two beds. We can try again in the morning."

Her eyes started to bulge, but Analese schooled her features with a stretch of her neck. "Okay," she replied. "I don't know why I didn't think of looking for a room while I waited. But my phone is about one click away from dying."

"You're not used to living in the sticks," he reassured. "I was thinking about it for most of the drive in. I had nothing better to do while I sat with him, so I took care of it."

Quicker than expected, the exit doors loomed ahead, and the night air whooshed in as they approached.

"I'm starving, so I know you are. Burgers okay?" Dalton asked as they passed through.

"Whatever you want," she replied. Without money, having an opinion about anything didn't feel right. She was simply a dead weight, and outside of being there when Martin's episode started, she served no purpose.

Dalton drove toward the hotel, stopping when he found a burger joint with the dining room still open. They placed an order and hunkered down in a booth until they had inhaled at least three bites before either spoke.

"So, you don't know his sister Matilda," Dalton began. "She's probably not going to get here for two to three days. That's her M.O."

Two to three days? Analese realized her mouth was open, and she was giving him a front row seat to the contents of her mouth. She closed it, swallowing then gulping down a mouthful of diet soda.

"Okay," she replied.

He chuckled. "It's not okay. I'd ask Van to come and get you, but with me out, he's really needed there to cover my shifts, and there aren't any buses that run that way. I'm afraid you're stuck with me. Sorry." He stuffed his mouth with a large bite, cheeks bulging.

"I'll manage," she quipped, licking ketchup from one finger before reaching for a napkin. She didn't mind being with Dalton, or in Nashville, or even in a hospital waiting room for three days. It was the lack of means to care for herself that ruffled her feathers.

"I've been thinking," Dalton mused. "Let's go find a thrift store, pick out a few days of clothes, then hit a laundromat."

"Tonight?" she balked.

He shrugged. "What else are we gonna do?"

She dunked three fries into a blob of ketchup as he sipped tea from an open paper cup.

"Sounds like a blast," she answered. "Do we have a theme? Or is it anything goes?"

There was a snort and then tea started running from his nose, and the entire restaurant watched as he half choked on his mouthful of food.

Analese fed him napkins, watching as his neat ponytail came undone in the process. Several minutes of spluttering later, red faced, and catching his breath, Dalton turned in the booth, placing his back to the wall and drawing his knees to his chest. He combed his lose hair behind his ears and cleared his throat.

His next words were just above a stage whisper.

"I'm sorry. That wasn't even that funny. You surprised me."

One brow lowered from her hairline. "What kind of theme were *you* thinking of?"

"Well, it's Nashville...so chaps might be involved."

It was her turn to laugh, and the stress of the day poured from her eyes in happy tears. She wiped them with the back of her hand, calming herself and licking her lips.

"I think I might be a little overtired," she confessed.

He sipped on his drink and nodded ruefully. "Same. Why don't we pack it up and get moving before all the stores close."

Agreeing, Analese took a few last bites before scrunching up all her paper and grabbing for the tray to collect their trash.

"You don't have to do that," Dalton complained, reaching for the tray.

She shook her head, snatching a wad of napkins from near his cup and adding them to the tray. "It's the least I could do," she insisted. "Let me do

120

something for you." Before he could protest further, she darted for the garbage can.

"Are you always this stubborn?" Dalton questioned as he carried his drink to the machine for a refill.

"No. I'm showing off," she retorted, joining him at the soda fountain.

He chuckled, pressing a plastic lid onto the cup. "Come on then, Brat. We've got shopping to do."

ELEVEN

THEY FOUND A THRIFT STORE open for thirty more minutes between their current location and the hotel he'd booked.

They hurried to the front door, and Dalton pulled it open wide for her. She brightened at the gesture before wilting under the rolling eyes of the employees as she scampered past him.

"Sorry, guys," Dalton apologized as he pulled a cart free of the others. "My uncle had a stroke this morning, and we got stuck here without any clothes."

"We'll be quick," Analese promised.

The pair of cashiers didn't bother to acknowledge them, leaning against the counter with their arms crossed. They looked tired, and Analese sympathized.

Dalton started toward an aisle. "Plan for three

days and don't forget PJs," he instructed.

"Got it," she called, making a beeline toward ladies' tops. Inside ten minutes, she was dumping her selections into his half-full cart.

"That everything?"

"Yep," she replied guiltily. She hated this feeling of being stranded and at his mercy. Not that he had been anything but generous and kind. But she felt like a free-loader, and she could pull her own weight for a little longer, unemployment notwithstanding. "Let me know what I owe you for this. Once I get the phone charged, I can send you money through my bank app."

His eyes scanned the cart. "You wanna grab a book or two for tomorrow while I get started checking out?"

The hours of staring at old magazines and sleeping on vinyl chairs made her neck ache, and the thought of entertainment widened her eyes.

"You're a certified genius!"

From the three shelving units of books in the back of the store, she listened to his southern drawl as he charmed the checkers while they rang up items. He shared how he'd gotten her call about Martin's stroke. Her cheeks burned as he praised her quick thinking to call him and their harrowing race all the way from Erin to Nashville to get him the care he needed. Without looking, she heard their sympathetic sighs and knew they were being forgiven for their late entry.

Deciding not to abuse their empathy, Analese grabbed three books that looked like they had potential and scurried to the register as Dalton laid a pair of plaid flannel sleep pants on the counter. She dropped her selections on the fabric, and the checker pulled them to the till.

"I didn't peg you for fantasy," Dalton commented as the checker priced each book. "Thought they'd all be trashy romances."

His smile looked like the start of a smirk to Analese, and she looked away from the pointed grin.

"Only to make Mary roll in her grave." She tapped her lip. "You make a good point. Maybe I picked wrong."

He laughed as she turned toward the books. "If you get through all of these tomorrow, I'll bring you back for some bodice rippers."

She squawked, clamping a hand over her mouth as the words washed over her.

Their cashier snickered before schooling her features. "I heard nothing," the woman denied.

Dalton glanced over his shoulder. "I should have grabbed a backpack."

"There's still time," the cashier encouraged.

Behind the counter was a grouping of items that appeared to be name brands with pink stickers lightly pressed on each. He squinted at the goods.

"What about that one?" He pointed to a floppy duffel bag with the word ADDIDAS in bold white letters across the side.

Following his gaze, the cashier lifted the bag in question from the rack behind her and passed it to him. "That's one of our boutique items."

Dalton unzipped it, inspecting it over several turns and giving it the sniff test. He turned the price tag over, frowning. "We'll take it. If you could put all our stuff inside, we'll save you a few bags."

The cashier brightened before giving him the total and loading their items. "You're a gem. I'm so sorry about your uncle," the woman soothed.

He acknowledged her statement with a nod and gave a wave of thanks to them both after the bill was settled.

Analese followed him back to the truck, studying his tall form highlighted in the warm yellow parking lot lights. The duffel bag was slung comfortably over his shoulder, and his gait was casual. Nothing about their whirlwind adventure in the thrift store seemed to have phased him. She recalled his words at the register, mentally recapping their day. It had been traumatic to say the least, and now here they were with no home and barely a room to their name, and Dalton was simply rolling with it.

"You're good at this," she commented as she buckled her seatbelt in the truck.

His brows wrinkled. "What do you mean?"

"In a crisis," she replied. "You don't freeze. You know exactly what to do. And you don't seem aggravated by the hassle."

Dalton revved the engine to life. "Martin didn't plan this. And he may as well be my uncle. It's the only thing I can do." He passed her the charging cable for her phone.

She plugged it in and sighed relief when the screen perked up, declaring 2% battery. The unfamiliar roads whizzing by as he drove seemed crowded compared to the last few weeks in Erin. Neon lights blinked over restaurants and pawn shops, spelling out most of the establishment's names.

"Has Martin ever had any scares like this before?" she questioned.

"No. His cholesterol number will freak you out, but he's always been healthy as a horse," Dalton answered without hesitation. "And I've known him forever."

"Maybe it's the new diet he was complaining about. All bland food."

Dalton's short bark of laughter filled the cab. "He would deem you his new favorite person for blaming that diet." He sighed. "Things happen. It's life."

His words sounded reasonable to her brain, but they didn't calm her heart. "Do you think he'll be okay?"

"I think he's too ornery to give up after a stroke. I

bet the old 'cuss will wake up in the middle of the night demanding to go home. Or a sponge bath."

Analese snickered at the thought. She could imagine it. "I didn't think you and Martin were related."

"We're not. Just close. He helped me through some rough patches."

She was dying to give him the third degree, mainly for amusement, but after the day they'd had, she decided it would be cruel. The man had, after all, fed her, clothed her, and was about to give her a place to sleep. The least she could do was allow him some modicum of privacy.

"I swear the nurses came to evaluate him every fifteen minutes," Dalton continued. "They kept saying all his vitals were improving. I don't know how anyone's supposed to rest through all that."

Words escaped her, and she shrugged sympathetically at him. They remained silent on the relatively short drive to the hotel. The scrolling sign boasted no vacancy, and they found a slip at the corner of the lot behind the building.

"I'll go get the keys if you want to wait here,"

Dalton offered, unbuckling his seat belt.

Analese wasn't sure she felt safe alone at night in this parking lot, despite how full it was, and she shook her head vehemently. "No, I'll come with. I need to stretch my legs anyway." She unbuckled and was out of the truck equally quick, both driver and passenger doors slamming at the same time. It took a light jog to keep up with Dalton's long stride.

She was stepping through the door as Dalton was announcing himself. The young clerk looked like he hadn't showered in several days, pushing his hair out of his glasses. His rosy cheeks stood out starkly against his pale skin, and she wondered if he had school in the morning.

There was a bare minimum of conversation as a credit card was exchanged and a plastic room key returned.

"Hey, is there a washeteria nearby that's still open?" Dalton asked as he slipped his credit card and license back into his wallet.

The kid shook his head. "No, but we got a washer and dryer down the hall you can use."

"Coin operated?" he pressed.

"Yeah, but I don't got any change. We don't really keep cash on-site." He slouched back in a worn, black office chair, beginning to twist from side to side as he picked up his smartphone.

Dalton nodded politely and stepped away. "Well, I guess we're in for the night. Except I need some change." He held the door open, then led her toward the truck. "I think I've got enough to start a load. Do you mind starting the wash while I go get change for the dryer?"

Analese nodded. "I don't mind at all. I even have a book to read thanks to my hero."

Dalton's eyes crinkled, and he scratched the back of his head as he opened the door to the backseat. "Don't go making my head swell. I still got some driving to do."

She chuckled as he handed over their duffel full of thrift store fare and the room key. He moved to the front of the cab, stretching his long body across the driver's seat and digging change out of the console.

"This should buy you one load and soap. I hope."

She held out one hand for him to deposit the loose coins. Her hand looked like a child's beneath long, slender fingers. She squeezed the coins tightly before shoving them into a front pocket, relieved not to hear any hit the ground in the dark.

He climbed in the driver's seat, and she started to back away, then remembered one last thing. She rapped one knuckle against the door and waited while the window rolled down. "Can I have the charging cable too?"

He shook his head. "It's like you didn't even know there was going to be a medical emergency when you went to Martin's office this morning."

"I know. I was thoroughly negligent," she agreed.

The single yellow light illuminating the parking lot caught on his broad smile as he extended an arm toward her, a white charging cable and plug dangling from his fingertips.

"I won't be long," he promised.

She shifted the bag on her shoulder and spun on one foot before heading straight to the laundry room, grateful to find two empty sets of machines. A fluorescent light flickered overhead. A vending machine in the corner held individual packets of laundry soap, fabric softener, and bleach in a variety of scents.

Her cheeks warmed as she dropped three pairs of men's underwear into the washer. She started the machines and plugged her phone into a loose wall outlet. A pair of plastic chairs were shoved against the wall, and she sank into one. The three books waited on the dryer daring her to dive in, and she turned them over trying to choose where to start. Within moments she was immersed.

When the washroom door popped open, Analese nearly launched out of her chair in startlement, dropping the book and cringing as it fell shut.

"Boo," Dalton said with a chuckle as the door closed behind him. He reached for the book, passing it back to her. "Must be something pretty... *interesting*...in there."

She frowned. "I think I ended up with a trashy romance book anyway. But with dragons," she confessed. She had been so shocked reading about a lascivious bath scene between two characters that she had forgotten Dalton would be joining her. "My mother would roll over in her grave if she read this."

"You should go read it to her in the cemetery and

find out."

A flush covered Analese's face, unsure if she could ever read these words out loud. While his suggestion had merit, she decided that avoidance was the most appropriate approach.

"Did you get the quarters?"

He held out a handful of warm coins and passed them to her.

"Have you been to the room yet?"

"No. I wasn't sure I was ready to brave that alone. Someone had to keep an eye on our valuables."

Dalton's lips quirked up as he dropped into the chair beside her. "Someone might see our Addidas bag and think we have something to steal," he chuckled and reached for one of her other books. "Is this one any good?"

Analese snatched it from him and clutched it her chest. "After the way this one went, I'm not sure I'm comfortable with you seeing that."

"And yet you're washing my underwear," he countered.

"Technically, they're not yours yet. They're from a stranger."

He arched a brow. "And this is less embarrassing?"

She shrugged. "I gotta draw the line somewhere."

He sighed, staring at her, arms crossed over his chest.

The gaze lasted long enough for Analese to squirm. "What?" she grumbled.

"After the day we've had, you're holding it together really well," he complimented.

She rolled her eyes. "You were right there next to me, having the same day."

"Yes, but Martin's like family to me. You barely know any of us."

"I don't have to know someone to have compassion for them. The man collapsed in front of me!"

"You haven't complained once about anything. I forgot to feed you for like eight hours, left you alone in an ICU waiting room without even a phone. And you're making jokes and washing used clothes so you have something to sleep in."

His words swirled around in her belly, and her skin puckered as she fought not to wrap her arms around herself. The first washing machine buzzed obnoxiously, and she jumped to extricate the wet load.

"I'm here to help. Like everyone in this community has helped me. Just because my mother did things to get things, doesn't mean that's how I think."

Dalton's smile did not fade, nor did his gaze.

She furrowed her brow. "Now you're making me uncomfortable."

He chuckled, unfolding himself and standing to his full height. "When I was out getting change, I picked up some breakfast and snacks. Help me carry them to the room?"

"Sure."

Laden with grocery bags, the pair traveled to the room with barely a word shared between them. Dalton swiped the key card and swung the door open. Inside was a pair of full-sized beds draped in what appeared to be shiny, quilted moving blankets. The chartreuse covers stood out starkly from the white walls. A bold painting stretched from one bed to the other, and Analese tried to ignore the obvious rip in the canvas over one of the beds. It drooped sadly, dust and cobwebs dripping from the edge that waved in the breeze from the in-room AC blasting beneath the plate-glass window.

Dalton whistled slowly, before kicking the door shut gently behind them. "I was going to offer to let you stay here tomorrow while I went to the hospital, but I think you'd better stick with me."

She nodded. "Which side do you want?"

"I'll take the one closest to the door."

TWELVE

DALTON EXTRACTED A BEER from one of the bags they'd carried inside and plopped on the edge of his bed. He took a long swig, and Analese watched as he drank, wondering how long he could go without breathing. She looked away when he stopped at half the bottle.

"I got you a couple wine coolers too," he offered.

"You remembered," she teased.

A soft smile curled his lips, and he glanced shyly at the floor. "I'm not always an asshole," he cited.

She frowned at him. "You're never an asshole. Ever."

He shrugged and took another pull from his bottle. "That's not what my ex said." Dalton lifted his hand. "Strike that. It's been a long day, and I'm a little morose after sitting in that hospital room all day listening to beeping monitors and breathing

137

machines."

"I heard nothing," she acquiesced, pulling a fuzzy navel wine cooler from the bags on the table.

"You were the real hero today, calling the police and me," he recognized.

She barked out a laugh. "Hardly. I stood there, watching him. He told me to call you. And you swooped in, grabbed him up, and raced all the way to Nashville, cool as a cucumber."

Dalton killed his beer and reached for a second. "He's like another father to me."

Analese waited for him to continue, but he didn't. She settled into her bed, tucking her knees to her chest as she sipped the citrusy peach beverage.

"Thanks for this."

He nodded. "After today, I assumed we both needed to relax."

"You're not wrong."

The rest of the evening passed in a blur, and they drifted off to sleep with barely a word.

In the night, Analese shifted, opening her eyes to see Dalton at the foot of her bed, smiling. He looked younger, somehow. At home. Sweet. A fuzzy feeling wrapped around her head, and she returned the gesture.

"What are you doing here?" she asked.

He shrugged, swirling a finger over her calf.

Her belly tightened at the sight of him wrapped partially in her blankets. She pulled the coverlet closer to her chest as she stared, strikingly aware that somehow in her slumber, her top had not only shifted but gone missing entirely. Only the coverlet was keeping her bare skin from prying eyes.

Dalton crawled closer to her legs, and she noted he wasn't wearing a shirt either. He draped one arm over her and rested his head on her hip.

She held onto the covers more tightly as they tried to inch down her body.

"I seem to have lost my top in the night," she explained.

Dalton shrugged, tugging lightly at the blanket.

She shrieked his name and clutched at the edge, raising up onto her elbows.

"Stop," she scolded. However, the giggle that accompanied her words made them ineffective.

Dalton met her eyes, then gave one more tug on

the blanket. It slipped from her grasp, exposing her chest to his hungry eyes. Her body warmed under his gaze, and her fingers curled against the bed. There was no point in hiding now. He'd already seen her unmentionables.

He crawled closer, his sleep warmed body easing gently over hers until he reached her face. Without a word, his lips brushed hers.

Even as it happened, Analese couldn't believe he was touching her. The moment his mouth touched hers, she gasped, returning the kiss.

He pulled back after a few gentle nibbles. "We've been divorced a long time," he rambled, words tumbling out of his lips in a torrent. "And we only married because she said she was pregnant, but she wasn't, and I couldn't get away any sooner."

Analese assumed he meant the ex-wife Van had told her about. His face was twisted with sincerity, pleading with her to forgive him. Accept him. She caressed his cheek, sitting up and allowing the blanket to slip. There was nothing to say, and she kissed him sweetly.

He sat up quickly, yanking the blanket completely

off her body.

Analese squealed, relaxed as he exposed her right down to her toes, only her panties leaving her any decency. She had expected to tense up, never having been seen naked before. Instead, she was calm, enjoying the way his eyes drank her in. She was ready, and in that moment, decided that whatever happened next was going to be the happiest moment of her life. She was going to enjoy every inch of him.

Dalton beamed down at her, immediately hooking his fingers in the sides of her underwear.

Analese squirmed, watching the fabric scrunch under his grip. This was going to happen. She was going to lift her hips and let him pull them free. But her bladder screamed.

"Wait, wait. Can I…well, I need to pee first. Is that okay?"

Chuckling, Dalton released the fabric and nodded, patting her thigh. "Of course."

She couldn't very well give into the lust if she had to pee. She scrambled from the bed, searching for the bathroom, but instead of the toilet she expected to see, there was a hallway. Everything came rushing back, and she remembered her father and Van were sharing the room across the hall, and they had a bathroom. She barged in without knocking, but Van was locked in the bathroom, and she snarled.

"What's wrong with you?" her father questioned.

"I really have to pee," she replied hastily. Dalton was waiting. There was no time to waste. One of them could lose their nerve, and those delicious kisses would be for nothing. And she wanted all of him.

She spotted a kitchen sink and without hesitation jumped onto it to relieve the urgent need to pee. "Sorry, dad," she giggled.

Needs abated, she darted from the room into a busy hallway. Where had she come from again? She rushed through the corridor, searching for her room, ascending and descending various flights of stairs, searching for the man who had seemed wholeheartedly consumed with the idea of removing her knickers. And she desperately wanted to let him and get on to the rest. But no matter who she asked or which way she turned, there was no way back.

With a gasp, Analese sat up in her bed, fully clothed, alone, and wide awake in a dark hotel room. She glanced at the other bed where Dalton was sound asleep on his stomach, facing the window and snoring lightly.

It was a dream. She sighed relief, closing her eyes. Remnants of the dream washed over her, and she felt his body sliding over her hips, his brown eyes unfocused and wanting as he pressed his soft mouth to hers. Tingles ran across her skin, and she touched her own lips at the memory. She could still feel him.

The sudden loss of his touch made her want to weep. What kind of crazy dream was that? And why couldn't she think of anything besides him nearly pulling her underwear off? The look on his face had been giddy. She had never seen that expression on him before. But if she hadn't been sitting on a hard mattress listening to him snore, she would have sworn it was real.

Throwing herself back down, she hid under the pillows. What if he knew? Had she really been having one of *those* dreams about the man across the room? Did she even have feelings for him?

Sex dreams were rarely about sex, she reminded herself, willing the goosebumps covering her to calm the heck down and go away. It must be the intimacy of racing to the hospital, doing their laundry, and watching bad movies till they dozed off. The dream had been intimate too, until the stress of losing him had taken over. And Dalton was a gentleman. He had given no indication that he had romantic feelings for her. He was simply kind, and her stress addled brain had interpreted that as sexual.

Consoling herself with the idea, Analese tried to go back to sleep. However, her bladder nagged at her that at least one of the feelings had been real, and she shuffled to the restroom.

THIRTEEN

ANALESE MADE HERSELF busy when Dalton showered the next morning. She heard the water bouncing off his wet body through the thin walls and cursed the builder. The dream rushed back to her, and despite having dressed already, her skin puckered at the thought of him naked in the next room.

He wasn't even terribly attractive, she grumbled internally. He was rail thin, and his hair almost touched his shoulders. Long hair on men had always been a turn off. His face wasn't just lean, it was gaunt. He was like a scarecrow, really. Never mind the fact that he was strong. She remembered all the things she'd seen him move like they were cartons of eggs. Things much heavier than she was.

Shaking her head, she grabbed her fully charged phone and two of the books. The naked man in the next room had no interest in her panties. They were stuck together by circumstance, not choice.

The water stopped, and she sighed in relief. On the table in front of her were the grocery bags still filled with snacks.

"Do you want to eat here or on the drive?" she called.

A moment later, his muffled voice answered through the wall. "On the road if that's okay."

"Yep!" she replied. She removed anything that wasn't a pastry and tossed the books in beside them. It was going to be a long day, and she hoped she would be able to focus on the paperbacks and forget the salacious dream that hadn't stopped plaguing her thoughts since she'd used the facilities that morning.

When the bathroom door opened, steam rolled out followed by the man in question. The black button-down shirt he'd picked out at the thrift store looked like it had been cut for him. He'd tucked it into his jeans with his usual belt, padding barefoot to his bed.

Awkwardly frozen in the center of the room,

146

Analese tensed as he brushed past her to pull clean socks over his toes.

"Sleep okay?" he asked. "You were out pretty hard when I got up."

She had most certainly not been asleep when he'd gotten up. But she was glad her faking it had fooled him. "Yeah. Great. You?"

"Better than expected. I'm giving the beer the credit. I don't usually have two on a weeknight."

"You sure it wasn't that documentary on the rain forest we watched?"

He chuckled. "Whatever it was, I'm grateful." He tied the laces on his boots and stood. "Ready?"

She nodded, displaying her bag of goodies. "It's all the rage in Paris."

"Chic," he replied, jangling his keys.

They locked up in a flash and slipped into his pickup quietly. The ride was silent, and Analese stared out the window, trying to erase the dream from her mind. They wolfed down plastic-wrapped pastries between red lights.

Twenty minutes felt like forty as she avoided his face until they walked through the double doors.

"I'll go straight to the waiting room," she stated as they reached the elevator.

"Okay. I'll come get you for lunch or let you know if anything changes. You got your books?"

She held up the bag of empty wrappers and vintage tomes. "I'll read slow," she promised.

He chuckled. "Devour them. I'll buy you more tonight if you finish them."

Her throat closed briefly as he smirked at her. It was a challenge. Why? Her face felt hot like it was about to melt off her bones.

The elevator doors dinged and slid open.

Analese struggled for words as she stepped out ahead of him.

"See you at lunch," she squeaked. She scurried down the hall making a left from the ICU and sneaked into the waiting room.

She wasn't sure how much time had passed when she heard her name called and saw Dalton looming in the doorway, but half the book was behind her thumb.

"He's awake," he announced. "He asked to see you."

Grabbing up her books, Analese trailed after him, barely keeping up with his long stride.

"Is he okay?"

"I think so," Dalton said, slowing his gait. "Or he will be. He's pretty rough at the moment, but he's coherent."

"And he asked for me," she clarified.

Dalton nodded, pushing open the double doors to the ICU. "I have to wait outside the room while you're in there. Only one visitor at a time."

"That's a dumb rule," she mumbled.

"It's a small room," he justified. "Thank God you're short."

"I'm not short," she snapped. "I'm very average, thank you."

Dalton looked down at her with his trademark grin and said nothing.

They stopped at Martin's door a moment later, and he held it open for her.

A nurse called to them. "Only one of you can go in," she ordered.

Dalton nodded. "We understand. I'm waiting in the hall."

"I guess chivalry isn't dead," the nurse mumbled.

Analese chuckled as she ducked inside the room. The same tubes and wires she had seen in the ER seemed to have multiplied.

Martin looked like a stranger in the lopsided hospital gown. His usually well-groomed white hair formed a messy cloud over one ear while the top of his head had gathered in greasy clumps. A thin tube was taped on his cheek and ran under his nose. A tank on the wall behind him hissed, and his breathing looked labored.

"Hi, Martin," she murmured. "You wanted to see me?"

The older man looked up with a grunt. "Yes. I wanted to thank you for getting me here."

"Oh, that was all Dalton. I'm afraid I'm not good in an emergency."

He grunted again. "He's a good boy. But I heard you on the phone. You spotted it right away. I might've been having a stroke, but I was still there."

She took a seat at his bedside. Dalton hadn't been teasing about the size of the room. She rubbed her palms over her knees. "How you feeling?"

"Peachy," he replied. "But I'm on the right side of the dirt. And that's on you, little lady. We're not done with that conversation about your mom's place. I'm going to figure something out."

"Oh, you don't need to worry about that, Martin. You've got bigger fish to fry."

"Eh, better than all this medical talk. I'm gonna be here for a while. They're talking about pacemakers."

"Oh, Martin, I'm sorry. But there's been so much advancement in medicine, I'm sure they do it all the time."

"But not from grade school. This kid they've got looking after me hasn't even hit puberty yet."

"Oh, that can't be true."

"Sure it can." He coughed several times till Analese thought a lung might fall into his hand, and a nurse rushed into the room.

"Mr. Russell, you need to settle down. We need to keep your heart calm. You've just suffered a major stroke."

"I know," he groused. "I haven't eaten since yesterday, and no one's brought me food, so forgive me for getting a little cranky."

"I'll see what I can do about that." She studied his monitor and checked one of the bags dripping into an IV tube. "You've had a big day. Why don't you get some rest, and I'll see what I can do about lunch."

The nurse's eyes narrowed in Analese's direction.

"I'm sorry. I'll go."

Before she made it all the way to her feet, Martin grabbed her hand with surprising speed.

"Seriously, kid. Thanks." He squeezed her hand as he met her eyes.

"It was my pleasure," she whispered, nose itchy with tears threatening to blur her vision. She squeezed him back and turned to go.

Dalton was resting on the wall, drumming his fingers against the railing. He straightened up, looking at her expectantly.

"He wanted to thank me for calling 911."

"Ah. How do you feel about lunch? After that stellar round of sugar this morning, I think it was our growling stomachs that woke him from his coma."

She chuckled. "So what are you going to follow that up with?"

152

He shrugged. "Let's take a walk and see what's nearby."

After her morning sitting in the waiting room, a walk sounded like a great idea.

FOURTEEN

THEY ENDED UP AT A TABLE service restaurant, and Analese added thirty dollars to her mental tab. The restaurant was crowded but managed to seat them within five minutes at a two-top table along the back wall.

"I'm so grateful that Martin's awake," she began once they'd placed their orders.

"Me too. That was a long time not to know."

She agreed. "He says they're talking about surgery for a pacemaker. That sounds serious."

"It is, but it's an outpatient procedure. Not like a bypass or anything. Don't let him scare you more than you already have been. I was there when the doctor saw him this morning. He'd been awake for about an hour before he asked to see you. I'm sorry I didn't get you sooner, but there was a lot going on, and I felt like I needed to be there."

"You need to stop apologizing to me. I'm the town interloper. I was in the middle of fantasy world hoping the twins could prevent war in the kingdom."

He chuckled. "How's it looking?"

"Grim," she replied as their drinks and salad arrived. She drank down her water greedily, not realizing how thirsty she'd been until the cool liquid filled her mouth. "Any word from Martin's sister?"

He replied with a full-blown laugh this time. "Yes. She'll get here at midnight day after tomorrow and expects me to meet her at the airport and bring her to Martin."

"Geez," she gasped. "Are you supposed to book her hotel to and take her to and from?"

Dalton snorted. "I wouldn't put it past her, but no. She told me she'd booked the hotel then asked me to run by and make sure it looked safe."

"You're joking right?"

"I wish I was."

Analese stabbed at her salad. "Is she somebody we should know? I can't think of any famous Matildas."

"No. She was the surprise baby in the family, and

the girl, so their parents raised a princess."

"I used to think that was a good thing, but I feel very wrong about that now."

Dalton chewed on his salad, but the corners of his mouth quirked up. After he swallowed, he changed the subject. "You'll be heading home soon, won't you?"

The happy tone of his voice brought a frown to her lips. "I suppose so."

"You must be looking forward to your own bed and surroundings. That trailer park is depressing."

A soft chuckle preceded her reply. "You'd think so."

He leaned closer, swirling the ice in his cup. "You don't think a group of people waiting around to die in tin cans is depressing?"

"When you put it like that…" She gulped back the warm sensation flopping around her belly at his nearness, and she was back in the dream, waiting for the moment when he would crawl up her body to kiss her. She could practically feel his soft lips against hers. Tamping down the feelings that were most certainly unrequited, she answered his question. "I won't miss Mary's trailer. I feel like I could catch something every time I lay down."

He smirked. "Mary's unit was always the most interesting. She always looked so surprised when something crawled up the wall while I was there."

Analese rolled her eyes. "As if she had no clue where all of them were coming from. I bet she even tried to make you feel guilty for not helping because she didn't even know how to get rid of them."

Dalton's only answer was an innocent and tuneless whistling sound.

Shaking her head, she patted his hand. "I hope you ignored her."

With a wink, he took a long drink of tea.

"I don't know. I don't want to be here, but I don't want to leave either," she confessed.

"You've decided Erin is the armpit you want to sniff for the rest of your life?"

A burst of laughter escaped her lips. "No thank you. Erin can keep its armpit to itself."

Dalton tapped her cup. "When did you slip vodka into this?" He sat back to continue his salad. "You're making drunk sense."

"I know." She sighed, worrying a napkin between her fingers. "Martin and Van and you…I'm going to miss you all when I leave. And I guess I'm not ready for that. There's a certain kind of…peace here."

"Awww…" he drawled.

"Don't aww me!" she scolded. "I'm serious."

"You can't live letting yourself be ruled by fear, speaking purely from a hypocrite's point of view."

"It's quiet here, which gives me a chance to think. I feel like I'm on hold here, but I also have nothing to rush home for." And she knew going home would spark an interrogation from her brother and father on any lurid tidbit she might have uncovered.

Reliving her past trauma as she emptied out the unit had brought with it a heavy bag of emotions. Things she had buried felt like fresh wounds again. While she appreciated the commiseration from her family, it was exhausting. They would want to hear about the mice and bugs and piles of mis-matched plastic containers. And then they would rehash her housekeeping skills. And with the recollection would come the lectures about how horrible a life she had lived and how put upon they all were, but most especially her father.

It wasn't new news. Like the trailer, she was ready to clean up and move on.

"So what are you going to do?" Dalton pressed. "You're not allowed to live there for another twenty years at least."

"Fifteen," she corrected. "But thanks for the compliment. And I would rather die under a bridge than live there, I think. But I can't make any decisions until Martin is released."

"You might be waiting for weeks. And I think Judy is stirring the pot to have Martin kick you out because you don't meet resident criteria."

Analese scowled. "That's ageist."

He shrugged. "If it makes you feel any better, they won't let Van and I live on site for maintenance either for the same reason, and we unclog their toilets."

"Gross!" She wrinkled her nose and pushed away her salad as she studied his amused expression. This is what she would miss. The crinkle at the corner of his eyes when he smiled and she could breathe again. Nothing could hurt her when Dalton was near.

What was she going to do in South Bend without

him?

His steady voice interrupted her train of thought. "Point is, you've got the place fixed up. You can do the rest by phone and email."

"If I didn't know better, I'd say you were trying to get rid of me."

He shook his head. "No, that's Judy. Not me."

"Liar," she teased.

"No, I'm not trying to get rid of you. I'm not sure you'd be happy in Erin."

"Probably not. I'm used to the stuff we have in South Bend."

He chuckled, spearing another bite. "Oh, you mean, like choice."

Analese smiled back at him. "There's nothing wrong with the Piggly Wiggly, but there's no competition."

"Sure there is," he countered. "If you're willing to drive forty-five minutes to the nearest Walmart."

"You're right. Forgive me."

He beamed at her as he relinquished his salad fork. "It's nice to have a fresh face in Erin. Especially someone my own age with stories I haven't heard."

"See, for me, you're all the new ones, and I haven't heard anyone's stories even once."

"You got a few weeks left before you'd run out, I promise." His tea was gone, and he tipped a piece of ice from the glass to his mouth to chew.

"Speaking of stories, Martin started to tell me one at the barbecue right after the whole incident at urgent care. About you."

His brows furrowed. "He's not one to tell stories about other people."

"Assume he took pity on me and was trying to make me feel at home."

"What did he tell you?"

"He said you should've been in Hollywood or Nashville. I guess he finally got you to the right place."

He frowned. "This is not the way to do it."

"We both agreed your music should be heard by more than people waiting around to die in tin cans."

"Oh, that." He took another piece of ice. "Martin's a nice guy trying to encourage me."

"I heard you too," she pointed out. "And you're talented. I'm no critic or anything, and I didn't know the song, but you were great. Confident and relaxed."

He folded his hands in his lap, staring at them as he replied. "Well, I wrote it, so I wouldn't expect you to know it."

Analese balked. "You're kidding!"

"Nope. I used to write in high school, and Martin gives me a few bucks to play at the monthly get togethers. And Van likes to show off, even for the grandmas."

"Well, now I'm all the way impressed." She swirled her straw in her glass. "So how come you're not playing big stages with girls swooning at your feet?"

His face scrunched up. "That's not me."

Analese squared her thumb and index fingers and studied him as though through a camera. "I dunno. I think with a little haircut, maybe a shave…you got something."

He pushed her hands away and picked up his empty cup, reaching for more ice. "Don't make a big deal. People write songs every day. That doesn't make them special."

"Sure it does. I can't carry a tune in a bucket let alone write the song, the lyrics, and then play and sing them with a partner. You're blowing my mind, and you're not even performing. You don't seem like the chicken type, so what's the deal?"

He shrugged. "Talent doesn't equal success. A lot of things have to line up just right to make the purse strings open up and radio stations take note. It's nothing more than a hobby."

"Hmmm," she assessed. "If you say so."

"But it's good to know you think I'm pretty," he teased.

"Was that tea from Long Island?"

"If only," he replied. "That would make today so much easier."

Before she could press him further, their entrees arrived, and Dalton veritably flirted with the waitress as he requested a refill on his tea.

The chicken piccata before her that had sounded so appealing when she read the menu now looked a lIttle sour. She poked at it with her fork.

"Well this looks delicious," Dalton admired, turning his plate till his meat was in front of him. He cut in without hesitation. "Pretty good for a lunch special."

"Sure," she agreed. At least the chicken was a distraction from all the emotions coursing through her system. The dream she'd had where she'd been ready to give him all her goods was nothing more than a dream. If he wanted to flirt with the waitress, that was none of her business.

She remained quiet as they dug into their food.

"Do we need to go grab you another book?" Dalton inquired after a moment.

"Neh, I'm good. I'm only half-way through the second one," she eschewed, taking a drink of her water.

"Well, rats. I was picturing Mary rolling over like a rotisserie all day."

At this, Analese started to choke, and she felt water trying to spurt from her nose. She stuffed her napkin over her face to cover the mess and swallowed awkwardly before squeaking, "Dalton!"

He leaned in with a smirk and lowered his voice. "They're all…a little trashy?"

"No! They're…well…"

164

He sat up, rolling his eyes. "What are you embarrassed about? The woman's dead. And who doesn't like a torrid affair every now and again?"

Analese's face heated at the suggestion, and she stammered.

Dalton sighed. "I thought you were a rebel."

Her mouth snapped shut as she mulled over his words. "I didn't say I wasn't."

His mouth split open from ear to ear, as he leaned back. "There you go."

FIFTEEN

Analese and Dalton took turns sitting with Martin until the nurses kicked them out at the end of visiting hours. Mostly, Martin dozed off and on, grumbling each time the nurses came to check his vitals. He saluted Analese where she stood outside his door, calling his goodnights to her obnoxiously.

To their credit, the nurses paid him no attention.

"He is a character," Analese murmured as she and Dalton waited for the elevator.

"Don't encourage him. We have enough character around the park."

She smirked. "How is the park, anyway? I assume you've been staying in touch with Van?"

He nodded as the doors slid open. "Same as always."

The walk to the truck was silent, and the

slamming of the driver's door echoed in the parking lot as Analese buckled her seatbelt.

Dalton slipped the key into the ignition but turned his eyes on her without turning the key. "Do you play pool?"

"Not really," she replied.

"Want to learn? I'm not sure I can stomach sitting in that room another night."

She studied his face. His face was relaxed, hopeful even. "Sure, okay. I'll try, but I can really only promise to be horrible."

"Good! I could use an easy win. How do you feel about greasy food?"

"Will there be salt and soda too?"

"Absolutely!"

"Then I'm in," she agreed.

Dalton's grin lit the cabin of his truck as he started the engine. With a few taps on his phone, his GPS was navigating the streets of Nashville directing them toward a nearby pool hall.

Analese smirked at the way his body had transformed from maudlin to gleeful with the mention of a single word. "I had no idea you were such a pool shark."

He chortled. "Hardly. But it's good, clean fun that'll keep us entertained. I don't know about you, but do not relish the thought of another documentary."

"Oh, you don't know. We might've found a movie from the eighties to mock."

"Let's not risk it," he replied.

The car was quiet for a minute before curiosity got the best of Analese. "So how good are you?"

"Fair to middlin'," he answered. "Van and I used to play a lot as teenagers. Got into a fair number of scuffles over it, too. Van's pretty great at it."

"Hustling at a young age, I see."

Dalton nodded enthusiastically. "Lot of money in illegal pool. That's why we're both living the high life now."

She snickered under her breath. "So what you're saying is that after a peppy music montage, tomorrow night we can go hustle back all the money I've cost you since we got here?"

"Yes, that's exactly right," he quipped. "In fact, the student will become the master."

168

Shaking her head, Analese returned to studying the unfamiliar streets, mouth watering at the thought of a cheeseburger and fries or onion rings or whatever other bar food available at the next stop. When he pulled into a parking lot of a strip mall, Analese cast a concerned glance his direction. Several of the letters over the pool hall's door were either missing or dark. The parking lot was full of low-end cars, some running on spares and rust.

She wanted to question him, but Dalton wouldn't take them anywhere he felt unsafe. Casting a wary eye at the dark windows and neon beer logos, she screwed up her courage and hopped out of the cab with him.

Dalton's lean frame nearly swaggered as he approached the door, holding it open wide for her.

The building's interior did nothing to allay her fears. The walls were covered in two colors of brash paint, maroon on the top, and black on the bottom. However, the colors did nothing to detract from the pock marked walls. Fluorescent lights overhead cast shadows over years of scars marking past games gone wrong. However, the room was filled with eight pool tables dividing the room into four sections where a pair of pool tables sat perpendicular to the next pair.

At the far end was a massive wooden bar surrounded by patrons in jeans and black T-shirts or leather vests and jackets. A few high-top tables punctuated the space between tables.

Dalton wasted no time claiming an empty table in one corner of the establishment. He tapped the corner, waiting for her to catch up, then passed her a stick. "Wait here. I need change."

"You just summed up the entire trip."

He smiled then stuck out his tongue at her before weaving through the crowd to a brown change making machine near the bar.

Analese practiced holding the cue stick, aiming it down the length of the table. She caught Dalton watching her as he returned and struck a silly pose. The moment she twirled the pole toward the ground, it slipped from her fingers, clattering and bouncing twice before she could grasp it again.

"I meant to do that," she swore when he was close enough.

170

He nodded. "I felt sure you did." He fed quarters into the table until the sound of billiards releasing into the end of the table made Analese jump.

He pulled a rack from the wall and tossed it in front of him before dumping the balls into the triangular plastic form. "I assume you know the basics. You use the stick to hit the cue ball which then knocks another ball into the pocket. Solids or stripes. Sink the eight-ball last."

She nodded. "Yes, I remember playing when I was little at a campground once or twice. But we didn't usually have the time or quarters to play."

He settled the balls into the frame and pushed it around the table a few times before sliding it to the middle and removing the rack. He placed the cue ball on the table and held out one hand. "Would you like to break?"

She frowned. "I think that's a bad idea. Why don't you get us started?"

He arched a brow, then shrugged. "If you insist."

Dalton maneuvered to one end of the table, checked behind him for people, then bent low across the table. The cue was an extension of his body, and within the space of a breath, he let loose one tap to the white ball in the center. Solids and strips scattered, their cracks echoing off the walls. One red and one blue ball fell into different pockets.

"I guess I'm stripes," she murmured.

He smirked.

"Is this the part where you clear the table before I get off a single shot?"

"No. I just got lucky." He bent over the table again, and her eyes covered him in an instant. The way his elbow pointed at the drop ceiling, and one hip tilted slightly up, jerking as he took his next shot.

The balls cracked and scattered across the table, bouncing, but none of them disappeared.

Exhaling nervously, Analese turned her cue in her hand. "My turn," she announced happily. At least, that's how she hoped she sounded.

She licked her lips, attempting to mimic his posture as she bent over the table.

"You can move the white ball if you want," he offered.

"I know," she replied. "But I like it where it is."

Analese wasn't sure that was true. However, she

had no idea where else to put it, so she eyed the balls where they sat. A striped, purple ball sat near the corner pocket, and she thought she had a slim chance of knocking it in. She practiced moving the cue against her thumb. It felt unstable, but she had no idea how to fix it. In all her staring at his last two shots, she hadn't thought to watch his hands.

Sucking in a breath, Analese aimed, closed her eyes, and shoved the stick at the ball. A clacking sound alerted her that something had gone wrong, and her eyes snapped open, watching the cue stick jump over the white ball and smack into the eight ball several inches away from her target.

Dalton's snort nearly covered her own hiss as she cringed away from the table, clinging to her cue for dear life. She wanted to tell him how embarrassed she was, but he had seen the shot. He was probably having replacement shame for her right now.

Dalton snickered. "Do you want to try again? I'll give you a freebie."

She groaned. "I'm not sure I should be allowed near the table again. What if I tear a hole in it?"

He snorted. "Unlikely. Look, why don't I give you

a few tips? If no one's ever shown you how to hold the cue, what makes you think you would know? It's not as obvious as it seems."

"I'm not sure I'm teachable," she groused.

Moving around the table, Dalton scooted the eight ball back into place and then picked up the cue ball. "Let's try again. It's more fun if you have an idea of what to do." He placed it on the table. "You in?"

With a sigh, she answered. "I promise to try."

"Good."

In a flash, Dalton was in front of her, prying the cue stick from her hands. "First rule: don't have a death grip on the stick. It should almost float in your hand." He demonstrated moving the cue in his palm, thumb down, and for a moment, Analese was transported back to her lascivious dream, and she imagined something other than a cue stick in his hand. She gulped, cheeks burning as she nodded her understanding.

"Next, you're allowed to touch the table. You seemed really unsure about the cue resting on your fingers, so there's a way to make sort of a hole with your fingers so you have more control."

174

The word pricked her brain. Control. She imagined he might have amazing control. She blinked, mouth dry. "Yes, that sounds much better. Show me," she requested.

He fumbled, trying to make the shape in the air, but then gestured her to the table. He placed his palm on the green surface, forming the shape with his fingers. "Like this."

And suddenly, all she could see was the stick penetrating the hole. She cleared her throat. "Okay. Got it."

Dalton straightened, passing her the stick. "Last rule is to try to keep your elbow at a ninety-degree angle to the table when you line up your shot. So where you are at the table and how close you are to the ball will determine where you hold the stick."

She shook her head. "That's a lot to remember."

"I have faith," he promised. "Go ahead and try. And if you don't get one in, no big deal."

She chuckled. "Let's not pretend you're not going to wipe the floor with me."

"You never know," he encouraged.

Analese bent over the table, closing her eyes. She

had to focus on the task at hand. This time, she moved the cue stick gently, practicing what he'd instructed. "Better?"

"Very promising," he praised. "Now give it a little tap."

After one more practice motion, she released the cue stick against the ball. This time, it struck, but with almost no force. The white billiard tapped its target and moved it a half inch away from the pocket.

"Well, it's progress," Dalton consoled. He moved past her, taking the cue ball and placing one more in the pockets before scratching.

He placed the cue on the table for her. "Okay, I'm going to give you just a little more and then you're on your own."

"I'm a lost cause, am I?"

"No, but you're also not a charity case. And I can't have you catching on too fast."

"Am I sure you're the right one to help? You did just scratch."

He held up his hands on protest. "I don't have to try to help," he quipped.

She shook her head. "No, no. I need all the help I

176

can get."

He winked, nodding as he moved to stand behind her. "Okay, we're aiming for 13 with the orange stripe," he instructed. "I'm going to show you how to give it enough power without sending it flying across the room. It's something you learn by feel."

Her eyebrows shot up and in as she interpreted his guidance.

"Go on. Bend over like you're going to shoot," he ordered.

She gulped, looking away from him and leaning down onto the table.

In the next moment, Dalton was pressed behind her, pelvis to pelvis, his right arm wrapped over her back to reach the cue. His breath wafted against her ear as his hand covered hers over the cue. "Not too tight. We're going to try it in slow motion first. Pull back, swing forward." He moved her hand backward and forward as he spoke.

"Line up the cue with the ball. There you go."

And suddenly, he pressed her arm forward. The cue connected with the ball, a lightning crack sounded, and the white ball went flying toward its goal. Number thirteen went sailing across the table, tapping against a bumper and then landing in a side pocket.

Dalton stood up behind her to cheer, the warmth disappearing immediately.

"And that's how it's done."

A shiver ran down her spine, and she stood to face him. "Wow!" she exclaimed. "That means it's my turn again?"

He nodded. "Until you don't sink one. But I think we both need drinks. You were so tense. I think you need to loosen up."

A laugh sputtered from her lips. "Yes, that sounds like a great idea. Can I have something sweet?"

"Absolutely."

Analese stared at the table, the balls randomly scattered across the surface. None of the striped balls were near a pocket, and she frowned, trying to determine where she might have the best chance to sink another billiard. The seventeen ball was possibly the only shot she had, and she mentally prepared. She should take the shot while no one was looking, but it felt like cheating.

She turned to see him at the bar, gesturing to the bartender then leaning against the edge as the drinks were prepared. He seemed perfectly at home between two other patrons, one toe perched on the brass railings. His legs looked like they were a mile long, the tips of his boots pointing toward liberating libations.

She turned away, chalking the tip of her cue stick to give herself something to focus on other than the length of his limbs. Because if she didn't, she would be dreaming of how long they felt slipping over her body in her dream. Why was she obsessed with it? It was just a dream! And a dream she should be ashamed of, no less.

Dalton returned quickly, holding out a plastic cup to her. "Whisky sour, as requested."

"How much did this set me back?"

He rolled his eyes. "You're lucky. It's girl's night. Free."

She looked around the bar. "I don't think it's working."

He snorted. "Okay, drink up and take your shot. I wanna see the moment when the student becomes the master."

Analese gulped half her drink, bent over the table, lined up the shot and swung her arm. The cue ball struck, and while she completely missed the mark, another striped ball bounced against the bumper, shot across the table and landed in a corner pocket.

"Holy smokes! You actually did it!" He held up his hand for a high five.

She jumped an inch to smack her palm against his, beaming at him. "I should quit now. It can only go downhill from here."

"No. You've tasted success. Slurp it up."

Cackling, Analese nearly jabbed herself in the face with her cue stick as she clamped a hand over her mouth. "Slurp it up?" she repeated.

He shrugged. "I stand by it," he replied, chuckling.

She snickered and turned to the table again. Eyeing the table, she picked a ball and took aim. The ball ricocheted off the side pocket before slowing to a stop between two others.

"Well, I had a good run," she consoled herself.

He grinned. "Drink up. You'll either play better or

be better. You win either way." He twirled his stick between his fingers and circled the table.

Analese snorted again as she took another drink. It might have been an unpleasant color of fall leaves, but the drink was sweet just as requested. After one more sip, she was surprised to find only ice left in her plastic cup. She rattled the ice, looking for the rest of it.

"Not fair, making noise as I'm about to shoot," Dalton groused, standing up from the table.

"I'm sorry, are we playing golf? Everyone around here is ignoring you. I think I should follow their example."

He rolled his eyes but followed up with a grin before taking his next shot.

By the end of the evening, Analese summarized their outing in terms of how many balls she'd sunk total versus game wins or, rather, losses. Dalton had easily won every game, but Analese didn't care. Her prize was watching his body contort over the table to hit the more difficult angles.

He wasn't skinny, she realized. More athletic and...lithe. Sinewy. And with every free lady's night whiskey sour she consumed, the more interested she became in each pop of his hip into the air as he balanced his shots. And the longer she ogled him, the more she thought about the sexy dream of him sliding up her body. No one seemed to notice or treat her any differently. She chewed her bottom lip happily as she downed the last of her drink.

As he sank the latest 8-ball, she placed one hand on the table to maintain her equilibrium. "Congratulations. The master has remained the master."

"What do you say we pack it up, and I'll catch up to you with the drinks in the room?"

She giggled. "I'm glad one of us showed some restraint." She thought that's what she said but stumbled over the last word.

If Dalton noticed, he didn't let on as he escorted her to the truck and closed her in once she was seated. She struggled setting the buckle in its latch. It clicked into place as the driver's door opened, and Dalton joined her.

He pulled away silently.

"That was fun," she complimented. "And I was

better at the end, just like you said."

"Good. I forgot about the hospital for a minute at least."

She frowned. "Me too. I should feel guilty about that."

"No. You gotta take a break."

Analese watched the streetlights blur as he drove, squeezing her eyes shut as he took a corner. "If my mother knew that I spent the evening in a pool hall drinking with a man..." She let the words hang in the cab between them.

"What? What did you do that was wrong?"

"Drink!" she exclaimed. "Big no-no."

"Because you're underage? Because why?"

She thought over his words for a while. "I don't know."

Analese was silent the remainder of the drive. Why was she so full of shame?

SIXTEEN

ANALESE HELD THE WINE cooler tight to her chest, curled into herself in the center of her bed.

"What'd I tell you? Perfect 80s B movie that you've never heard of and makes no sense at all." She pointed one pinky at the television.

Dalton tossed a beer cap in the direction of the trash can but missed by a few feet landing silently beside the first one. "You were right."

"We only missed the first, like, twenty minutes. And we'd have missed less if you hadn't taken so long in the bathroom putting on that." She waved a finger around him in the air, eyeing his white V-necked T-shirt and flannel sleep pants. "Can we watch it?"

"Knock yourself out," he replied, taking a long pull from his bottle.

"Thank you!" she squealed. Satisfied that she had

won some sort of battle, Analese stretched out her hands, sliding her whole body forward till she was face down on the bed, swinging her feet back and forth as she watched the tiny screen.

She started questioning the plot, calling out each tiny flaw. When he didn't answer, she frowned, peering at him from between her fingers around the bottle in hand.

"You're very quiet," she accused. "I see you over there catching up on pre-paid beer."

He shrugged. "I can't help being fiscally responsible."

Her lips contorted into a smirk. "Haven't you ever made up your own movie commentary?"

"Can't say as though I have."

"I pronounce that you are the one with the fucked up childhood." As the words left her mouth, she gasped, burying her face in the sheets. "I meant messed up."

He chuckled. "How do you figure that? Because I didn't mock someone else's art?"

Analese pouted for real, sitting up. "I'm not sure this qualifies as art," she countered.

"That's in the eye of the beholder. Someone wrote this, costumed it, filmed it, edited it, and set it to music. It's fun at least, even if it's not perfect."

"Drink more. You're making too much sense." The AC kicked on, and she felt a breeze on her belly, and she tugged down her shirt.

"You don't drink often, do you?"

She arched a brow. "You don't know." She took a long, rebellious drink from her bottle, fighting against the million tiny bubbles filling her stomach. She scrunched her face, and before she could work out what was happening, an enormous belch blared from somewhere near her pinky toe up through her sternum and out her lips followed by a series of follow up burps like aftershocks in an earthquake.

Analese's vision unfocused.

At this, Dalton fell back to his bed laughing, spilling his beer. When he finally settled down, he sighed. "I think you should probably go to bed. We can take these back, and you can have one final blow out before you go back north."

She sighed too. "I don't want to go back. Not if you and Martin and Van aren't going with me."

"Did you go catch feelings?"

"Feelings?" she repeated. "No. You're just…nice to me. And you three take good care of me."

"Your family's not nice?"

She barked out a laugh. "You met my mother." She frowned, thinking of her words. "No, they're nice to me. They take good care of me. Oil changes, lawn mowing. All the boy things."

"Boy things?" he laughed. "Are there boy things?"

"You know…lifting stuff, moving stuff, unclogging toilets."

"Your very own Boris Brothers at your service."

She pointed at him with one index finger and tapped her nose with the other. The cheesy movie on the television caught her attention. "I'm going to watch the movie. I even promise to be nice."

"I believe you," he replied.

Without the mocking commentary she had initially planned, the movie was actually quite dull. It wasn't until the next morning that she realized she'd fallen asleep.

The remains of her fuzzy navel wine cooler were warm, sloshing at the bottom of the bottle. A good portion of the drink had dried on the collar of her shirt, and the overly sweet smell turned her stomach. The TV was off, and Dalton's bed was empty.

On the bedside table was a cup of water and a travel-sized packet of ibuprofen. She struggled to get the pills out of the foil envelope, but the moment they were free, she guzzled water to wash them down stopping when the last drop glided over her tongue.

The white noise in the background suddenly stopped, and she realized that Dalton had turned off the shower. Her brain tried to twist around the idea that her friend was naked again in the next room, but the pounding of her blood rushing past her ears derailed the train, and she groaned into her pillow. A small burp escaped, and she cringed, remembering the one that had reverberated through the hotel room the night before.

At least the dream had been nice. After her drunken rudeness, he would never see her as a lady. And at any rate, she'd be heading home any day now, the threat of the trailer bill looming over her head. She'd always have her fantasy.

188

Steam rolled out the bathroom, and Analese heard the door open slowly.

"Matilda got in last night and used a hotel shuttle. Martin's called to let me know she's arrived."

Analese peeked an eye open toward the sound of Dalton's voice and was immediately transfixed at the sight of him. Loose tendrils of Dalton's hair escaped the hotel towel as he scrubbed it over his scalp. His button-down shirt hung open, revealing his body beneath it.

As torsos went, it wasn't the most perfect specimen she'd seen, but it was the first unclothed one she'd seen at her the foot of her bed.

"Okay," she mumbled.

Her own voice felt like an explosion in her skull, and her eyes closed as she gasped for breath.

Dalton's chuckle was faint but not silent. "I see you took the water and ibuprofen. Thought we'd have a good hangover breakfast before we face Matilda."

Her stomach knotted, and she had trouble distinguishing hunger from nausea.

"Shower's free if you wanna get ready. We're

checking out today."

She'd never drank enough to be sick the next day, and she wasn't sure why she'd allowed herself to keep drinking. She hadn't been raised to indulge. In fact, it was only in the last decade that she'd allowed herself to drink alcohol at all. Dalton's lack of commentary on her current state was startling. He hadn't scolded her once.

Being with him at a pool hall, she'd lost track of how often he'd refilled her cup. Why she'd opened a wine cooler upon their return was unfathomable.

Her collar and a section of hair was sticky with the residue of the sugary beverage, and it proved enough motivation to push her into the privacy of the bathroom with the rest of her thrifted wardrobe.

Was Dalton aware she was getting naked? She froze with her sleep pants at her knees, then rolled her eyes at herself in the mirror and continued undressing. The real question was if he cared. He'd been nothing but a gentleman since the day they'd met. And other than being friendly, he'd given no indication he was interested in her.

Was she even attracted to him? Or was he just

there? Convenient?

With a sigh, Analese pushed all the worry from her brain and chased it away with hot water and hotel shampoo. Her head relaxed its vice grip at her temples, and her body followed suit one muscle group at a time. By the time she emerged from the bathroom, she felt more like herself.

Dalton was stretched out in his rumpled bed, fully dressed and flipping through the beginning of one of her paperbacks. He tossed it to her bed.

"I've never been much of a reader. Seems like you are, though."

She nodded. "Spent a lot of time in cars as a kid, and my parents couldn't complain when I was quiet. It was a great way to escape." Analese stuffed her pajamas into their shared duffle and zipped it.

"I guess that's it," she announced.

Dalton agreed, standing and taking the bag. "Let's eat, make sure Martin's okay, and then head back."

"Sounds perfect."

By noon, they were headed back to Erin with full bellies and cloudy skies leaving Martin in his sister's hands.

SEVENTEEN

AN HOUR INTO THEIR DRIVE home, Analese's joints were aching from clenching in the passenger seat. It had started with dark skies, then a drizzle, and finally a downpour. She hung onto the door handle silently as rain pelted the ground around them. Everything in her was tense, and as a wave of water slapped the passenger window, she barely held in the surprise jump it gave her by clearing her throat. She glanced at the dashboard, noting their speed: 40 miles per hour. She could barely see the lines on the road separating the lanes.

The noise of the downpour had drowned out the radio close to twenty minutes ago. She shifted in the passenger seat, trying to think of something to say to alleviate the tension. But everything sounded trite, and she didn't want to distract him.

A gust of wind hit the truck, and this time, she

couldn't bite back a shriek. "Sorry," she murmured, gripping the door handle.

"It's okay. I'm a little freaked out too," he admitted. "If we have to slow down more, we'll be in park."

"Should we pull over?"

There was a long enough pause that she wondered if he'd heard her.

"I'm thinking about it. Except, I'm not really sure where we are, and I can't see shelter. Pulling over won't do us much good with these winds."

"Why not?" Analese panicked.

"Because we're in a truck."

"And? Aren't these things called half ton pickups 'cause they weigh half a ton?"

"There's nothing in the bed. We'd need weight to be stable, but we're empty. It's a real bitch on ice, but it's worse in a tornado."

"Tornado?" she repeated.

He nodded exactly once.

"If I see a shelter, I'll pull over. But we can't stay in the car. We'll have to make a run for it. If the truck goes end over end, I don't want to be inside."

Analese snugged her seatbelt and bit her lips together. Hadn't she been through enough recently after the surprise rescue mission to Nashville? Sharing a room with a man and stranded like a beggar for days? Karma owed her. She couldn't die now. Not yet. She was about to get started on her new life.

But that wasn't how karma worked. Deposits into the bank weren't intended as protection for the future. It wasn't insurance.

She took a deep breath and offered her prettiest smile at her driver. "You're doing great. I trust you."

Her breathing was shallow for the next five minutes as he persevered.

"Oh, shit!" he yelped.

She had barely registered the sight of half a tree blurring across the road ahead of them before Dalton slammed on the brakes.

Her seatbelt yanked her back as her body slid toward the front window.

The vehicle lurched to a stop as the other half of the tree and a four foot length of barbed wire fencing followed.

Dalton was a flurry of motion, one hand chasing the other around the steering wheel as he guided them to the shoulder and turned on the flashers.

Everything inside the cab was still as they caught their breath. She looked at his profile, checking for injury, but other than some loose hair around his face and his white knuckles on the steering wheel, he looked fine.

"If there's a fence nearby, there must be property. Can you see anything?"

Analese squinted out the windows, but it was nothing but a gray wall of precipitation and debris. The rain changed direction for a moment before slamming back into the window beside her ear.

"There," Dalton announced. "There's a barn."

She squinted in the direction he'd been looking, but she didn't see anything.

His seatbelt buckle clanged against the driver's door as he released it, and then he was on his knees, rooting around the back seat of the cab, mumbling as he did.

The thought of opening the door in this torrent terrified her. The rain would be cold. It would be in her ears, possibly up her nose. And if she couldn't see a barn ahead of them, how was she supposed to follow Dalton? Was he sure that staying in the vehicle wouldn't be the better option?

The man in question dropped back to the driver's seat, stuffing things into the pockets of his jeans, finally stuffing a two-foot-long pair of bolt cutters into one side of his waistband.

Dalton met her eyes. "This is going to suck, and you're going to be scared, but don't let go, and we'll be okay," he instructed.

She frowned at him but nodded.

"Scoot over to the driver's side. We'll both go out the same door. There's a ditch on the side of the road, and it's probably four feet deep. You'll get swept away immediately."

The thought of drowning hadn't occurred to her till he'd mentioned it, and Analese's stomach twisted into knots. Her mind spun in circles full of questions about how they were going to make it to this mirage of a barn he'd seen, but she put a lid on the worry. He had enough to deal with without her fighting him on his heroic efforts.

196

"You're sure we can't stay in the car?" she asked softly.

Dalton nodded. "I am. Leave everything behind. If we're safe, the cell phones are safer here, and we can call for help when it passes if necessary."

He stared at her, and Analese realized she had stopped breathing.

She gulped. "Okay. Tell me when."

He nodded, staring out the window and lightly gripping the handle.

Analese forced herself to take long, deep breaths as she scooted across the seat until their thighs touched. She did not want to be wet. She didn't want to be cold. Didn't want to be stranded for the second time that week.

"I think there's a break. Don't let go," he instructed swiftly, grabbing her hand. He pushed the door open, and the rain immediately sprayed her as Dalton jumped out of the truck.

His departure tugged her along, and she held her breath as she followed. As soon as her head cleared the cab, she was soaked to the bone. She wanted to scream, but there was too much water pelting her scalp and filling her ear canals. Sealing her mouth shut against the onslaught, Analese stumbled behind Dalton across the road.

He paused, poking at the ground with a tire iron. He was searching for a driveway, she realized, and squeaked with relief when he found one. The loose gravel was washing right over the toes of her sneakers as she scrambled behind him.

The going was slow, but to their good fortune, there was a break in the rain long enough for Analese to see the green barn with its snow-white trim ahead. She sighed relief, sucking in a breath with her chin tucked into her chest.

The rain caught its second wind in that moment, and Dalton's grip tightened. A few moments later, he took hold of her shoulders and pressed her against something firm: the barn wall. And then he let go.

Analese covered both ears, wrapping her arms around her head as the weather swirled around her. It felt like hours, but it couldn't have been, when a metallic snap made her body clench. Another slam followed the noise, but she recognized it as the door banging against the opposite wall.

Dalton's hands were on her again, dragging her inside the building.

The absence of the rain had her gasping for breath as she stumbled inside. An unnatural noise escaped her lips with each gasp. The fear she'd been keeping at bay wailed now, and she dropped to her knees, shaking.

Dalton was busy closing the door he'd just broken into, and when he finally secured it, the softening of the storm was deafening.

Tears coursed over her face. She wasn't sure if she was relieved to be safe again or terrified at what had just transpired. Either way, when Dalton wrapped her in his embrace, patting her back, the flood gates opened.

"We're safe," he assured quietly. "It's okay."

Analese sobbed for everything she was worth, until a litany of thank yous fell from her lips. She could barely understand herself, and she was sure he couldn't.

"Shh," he soothed. "You're okay. We're safe, but we can't stay this close to the door. It could blow open."

Pulling away, she wiped her face with her drenched sleeve, not sure it felt any better. "Okay," she complied, catching her breath. "I'm good. Let's go."

His hands moved to her shoulders, turning her and directing her deeper into the barn.

EIGHTEEN

THE DARKEST CORNER HAPPENED to be also the quietest. Flashes of lightning illuminated the way for the briefest of moments before booming seconds later. Overhead was the hayloft, and her ankles brushed against additional bales. Her eyes began adjusting to the dark, and she attempted to push her hair from her face.

Dalton had dropped to sit on the hay, running his hands over his head to slick back his hair.

After a moment's hesitation she seated herself beside him. The sleeves of her shirt were heavy, and she squeezed, listening to the water dripping out.

Wind and rain howled outside the building, and Analese tucked her knees up to her chest before she could get any colder. "You're sure this won't come down too?"

"Pretty sure. You don't lock up buildings if they're

about to come down," he reasoned.

"We're lucky you had bolt cutters in the truck."

"I had a crowbar too." Iron clanked near their feet.

"I think you're even more lucky you didn't cut anything off running with those things in your pants."

Dalton's laugh filled the space, and it didn't stop.

Analese, joined in, and a bout of giggles set in.

"In my pants," Dalton said, snickering.

She felt more than saw him tumble to one side as he began belly laughing. "I can't believe you survived the storm, Dalton," he yelled. "But sorry to hear about your dick."

Analese, squealed with laughter, allowing herself to lay back in the hay. "You can always adopt," she teased.

Dalton made a choking noise at this.

Thunder cracked overhead, and a fresh round of laughter kept them from talking for several minutes.

"Speaking of things in my pants," he finally mumbled when he could form words again.

Analese felt a shift in the pile of hay beside her and then he pressed something onto her lap. She scrambled to keep from dropping it.

"It's an emergency blanket," he explained.

She chuckled. "One of those silver things that looks like it came off a space shuttle?"

"The same," he agreed.

"Do they really work?" she scoffed.

"Never tried one, but I'm about to."

The sound of crinkling wrappers in the dark filled the space between the raging storm outside. It was surprisingly difficult to open the tiny packet in the dark, feeling for the plastic wrap and then differentiating between the wrapper and the thin polymer material of the blanket itself. It took ages to unfold the thing, and she draped it loosely over her head.

"Do you feel warmer?" he asked.

"Not really. You?"

"Me either. I'm just so...wet."

Analese felt the same. Keeping hold of the blanket, she let it fall to one side. Maybe once she'd dried out, it would be more useful.

"Ever had to abandon a vehicle before?" Analese questioned.

"Nope. Van's gonna be pissed if it flips."

"Won't he be more pissed if he loses his best friend?"

"He has the range to be both."

She chuckled. "You've known each other a long time."

"Just a lifetime, but who's counting?" He sighed. "His parents were...probably a lot like your mom."

She grumbled. "He deserves a hug or something."

"We take care of each other. My family sort of adopted him, and he got me through the divorce. It all comes out in the wash."

The word hung thick in the air, and Analese's head whirled with questions. They could be trapped here for hours. If she asked, and he was offended, it would make the waiting unbearable. Or maybe it would get him talking and help pass the time.

"Ever been married?" he asked.

"No," she replied softly.

"I don't recommend it," he countered.

"That bad?"

His answer came after a fair amount of

emergency blanket crinkling. "You go into it alright. You just don't…come out of it the same."

"So just your run of the mill trainwreck."

"Heh." The near chuckle was stark in the dark. "Ever heard of a hall pass?" he asked.

"Like in grade school?"

"No…in a marriage. You know…that one celebrity that you will never in a billion years ever meet and would never have an interest in you, but your spouse gives you a hall pass on the rare occasion that it would happen. And you agree that it would be okay to cheat for that instance only."

Analese balked. "People really do that?"

"Well…I don't know. But we'd been together since high school. Erin's not a big town. Not a lot of prospects here."

"You only need one right person. The size of the pool doesn't really matter."

"It didn't to me. But we used to sit around the campfire and talk about stuff like that. If Julie ever met Craig Coolidge, all bets were off, and I should understand."

"I don't know who that is," Analese interrupted.

"You live under a rock?" he teased. "He's huge in country music. Like massive."

"I don't believe country music is a thing. It's just noise," she teased.

He grunted. "I'm wounded, Ana. Wounded!" He chuckled before continuing. "So there we are in Nashville…cutting my demo. And there he was. Recording in the studio next to mine."

Her heart ached. She wanted to sling mud at the other woman for leaving a man as purehearted as Dalton. But she held her tongue.

"You think all that stuff is just nonsense. It's the beer. It's stuff immature kids say. When you've made a commitment to someone — taken vows… And then you think there's no way a major celebrity like that would ever come after your wife."

She pressed her knee to his without a word. Nothing she could say would take that away.

"Maybe it's best you never got married."

"Maybe," she agreed. "Easy to know you don't like something when you've had it. Harder to know you wouldn't like it if you've never tried it."

"True."

Analese's teeth chattered, and she swallowed it back.

Dalton scooted closer, and she felt his arm around her back. "I don't bite, no matter how nicely I'm asked," he offered.

She wanted to protest, but he was considerably warmer than she was. "You must regret ever meeting me. The first time you saw me, I was bleeding and needed a trip to urgent care. It's just gone downhill ever since."

"Yes, I have been thinking that everything that's happened since we met has been not just bad, but also your fault."

She laughed heartily. "Go on. I'm used to it."

"Well, since you offered, this is quite a storm you cooked up for us. Nice touch with the soaking wet clothes and abandoned barn."

She leaned against him. "Well, if I didn't have the opportunity to die without fulfilling half my life goals, I would've felt incomplete."

"Life goals?" he teased. "Tell me more."

Heat flushed her face, and she was grateful for the lack of light to hide her embarrassment. "Well, maybe goals is a strong word," she hesitated.

"Like what? I just told you about my divorce. Don't hold out on me now. It wouldn't be fair."

"It's really just personal stuff. You don't wanna hear about it."

"What else are we gonna do? We've shared a room for the last three days, and now we're trespassing. We're practically Bonnie and Clyde here with bolt cutters and everything."

She giggled, trying to cover the nervous shiver that wriggled from her shoulders to her toes. If she couldn't own her own thoughts to a near stranger in the dark, how would she ever move forward?

"I know my mom was like a pimp, trying to foist me off on any breathing male of any age, but she was never successful. Never managed to have so much as a date."

"That was hardly her job. And to be fair, it does make a girl sound desperate to the untrained ear."

She chuckled. "Whole societies were born out of arranged marriages." She grimaced. Admitting to never having had a date was bad enough, but to confess she'd never been kissed? Never even held hands with a man? She wracked her brain for another topic.

"And travel!" she exclaimed, citing another missed "goal" in her life. "I haven't made it to Australia yet!"

"Well if that isn't a reason to live…"

She snorted. "And I want to go back to Disney."

"In love with Mickey are you?"

Thunder cracked outside, covering her answer, and she nearly leapt into his lap.

"We should've grabbed the rest of the liquor," he sighed sadly.

"Yes. Much more sensible than bolt cutters."

"That's why I said it. We'd be getting waterboarded, but at least we might be wasted."

"Not off what we had left," she countered.

Electricity roiled in the air, and the hair on her arms started to prickle. "How long do you think this is gonna last?"

She felt him shrug beside her.

"Dumb question. Sorry."

"It's okay."

Words failed them both, and the sounds of the

storm filled the space between them.

She reached down and tugged at her shoes and then socks, trying to drape each cotton tube over her shoes. "I'm terrified of losing my shoes and socks in the dark," she noted. "But maybe my feet will be warmer if I can get them dry."

"That's a great idea." After a moment, she felt him press his blanket into her palms. "Hold this. I'm going to take advantage of the dark." He wriggled next to her, and she felt his arms lifting overhead. The next thing she heard was water dripping onto the ground a few feet away.

"Are you ringing out your shirt?" she quizzed.

"Yeah. It's pretty satisfying. You should try it. You'll warm up faster," he promised.

"Are you trying to get me out of my clothes?"

"Managed that days ago," he replied smoothly, taking his blanket back. "I just arranged for a good friend to have a severe stroke with you then rushed you to the hospital during a sold-out convention in Nashville. Piece of cake."

"Your wife was a fool," she mused. "You are the coolest person I've ever met."

Dalton said nothing, and in the awkward silence, she turned her back to him and pulled her shirt over her head. The air was like a freezer over her damp flesh, and she wrung the water out of her clothing as best she could.

She pulled the silvery blanket over herself to protect her decency, and it stuck to her shoulders. In moments she felt warmer, her body heat trapped beneath its shiny surface. If she had any sense, she'd throw her dignity out the window, strip down, and dry out in the dark. It wasn't like Dalton could see her, and the warmth spreading over her torso relaxed her body.

"I'm going to try to get a little sleep," she announced. "I'll just be here on the hay."

"Go ahead. I'll keep watch," he answered.

"You think we need to? No one's coming to find us in this mess."

"I'm not sleepy," he replied.

She waved a warm hand in his direction and made herself comfortable. Unconsciousness swept her away in bliss.

When she woke, she knew she wasn't dreaming.

It sounded like a freight train was barreling down on them. The walls creaked, but they held. Flashes of lightning revealed every broken board and crack in the building. And inches from her face, Dalton. His breath was hot against her forehead.

She blinked, staring directly into his brown eyes. His parted lips. The tip of his nose. All of him was focused on her. Her heart was racing in the moment, breath shallow and quick. She must've sounded like a scared rabbit.

At the next crack of thunder, his hand was on her cheek, pushing stray hair behind her ear. This was nothing like the dream in the hotel room. It was too real. The pulse of his fingers singed across her skin, and his eyes darted from hers to her mouth and back.

The hay sounded as loud as the thunder, crackling beneath the blankets. And his face scooted closer until their lips touched. The first contact was just a brush, and he pulled away. Searching for permission.

It didn't matter that the world seemed to be hurtling down around them. It didn't matter that they barely knew one another or that she was going home soon. What mattered was that they were here. Together. Now.

Analese kissed him back. She wasn't sure if it was shyly or aggressively. It was the first time she'd ever done it.

She was rewarded when his arms clamped around her, pulling her tightly to his body and kissing her back eagerly.

His skin seared hers, and she shut off her brain, drowning herself in the sensation of bare skin against her own. She ran her palms over his back, shuddering when her fingers stopped at the band of his wet denim waistband.

She wasn't sure how it happened, but he was guiding her fingers to the button at the front, and then he was kicking the jeans away.

They weren't just making out. Clothes were disappearing for reasons other than heat. Analese gave herself over to the desire pooling in her belly, following him deeper into the act.

Any of the shame she expected to feel at being naked with a man was gone. It was just them in the barn, trusting each other to do good and not harm. Feeling their way into an intimate connection. Giving each other life. Enjoying the pleasure of each other's company. As long as she could touch him, *feel* his touch, they were safe.

Neither spoke a word. They didn't need to. Dalton seemed to know exactly what she wanted and gave it to her without hesitation. In his arms, she felt natural. Feminine. Soft. And worthy.

NINETEEN

THE STORM MUST HAVE ENDED in the wee hours of the morning. But all Analese remembered was the sound of Dalton's heartbeat against her ear.

The inside of the barn was still mostly dark even with sunlight peeking through the boards. The space blankets had done a fair job of shielding her from the cold.

Daylight shone between the old boards, and she scanned their surroundings in the dim light. She was alone on the hay with her blanket clutched tightly around her naked body. Hay poked her side, and she shifted uncomfortably to get away from it.

Dalton was a few feet away attempting to put on his underwear while standing. She frowned as the black briefs covered his behind. Was this how the morning after happened? In the quiet, one person got dressed and didn't bother to wake the other?

Shouldn't there have been some tender words? Sweet nothings? At least an acknowledgment of enjoyment?

Of course, maybe they had clung to each other in some life affirming way. Maybe he thought they would both die in the night, and they may as well enjoy the comfort of each other's arms.

And it had been comforting. With Dalton so near, she couldn't be worried about the howling winds or creaking boards protecting them. The world had boiled down to the places their bodies touched. The volley of water and wind only took her caution with it, giving over to the sensations that were good and wholesome.

She fumbled to stand with the blanket clutched to herself then followed his lead. The first order of business was finding her clothing. Neither had been terribly careful undressing each other. She found her underwear first. They were damp and stuck to her legs as she tried to roll them up without letting go of the blanket.

"Here," Dalton grunted, holding his long arm out to her.

Her gray and pink polka dotted bra dangled from his fingertip, and he didn't meet her eyes as he waited for her to take it. "It was under my shirt."

"Thanks," she mumbled, snatching it from him. Turning her back to him, she dropped the foil blanket and slipped it over her arms. The bra was more than damp still and felt like ice against her warm, sensitive skin. She squirmed, biting her lip to hold in the shriek at the contact. It wasn't simply that the bra felt disgusting. It was that her skin was tender. As though someone had been man handling her body just hours ago.

She clasped the garment behind her back, every inch of her drawn back into those moments. Grateful for the lack of light, she scrambled to where her shirt was draped over an old barrel. Thankfully it was dry and slipped over her head without issue.

Her socks were dry, but the shoes were still wet, and while her jeans were dry, they were stiff and cold. She struggled to pull the denim over her warm body, but she managed without complaint.

Dalton was waiting for her to finish, and she felt his eyes on her as she tied her wet shoelaces. Was he mad? Had the sex been so bad for him that he didn't want to talk about it? It couldn't have been. She hadn't been the only one yelling ecstatically in the dark. But maybe that's how it was for guys? No amount of book reading, movie watching, or listening to her friends could've prepared her for what to expect the morning after this situation.

"I think we should go see what's left," he suggested.

He was still in survival mode, she realized. She stood and nodded, following him to the barn door.

It was eerily quiet as they exited the barn. After the screaming storm the night before, the quiet made her shoulders tense in the red morning sky. Not a single cloud shadowed the ground, and every remaining thing was still. Everything else was mud and tree roots. A heavy-duty tractor was half buried a dozen feet away.

She scouted for the side of the road where the full drainage ditches were racing downhill. Where was the truck?

Dalton stood stoically beside her, hands poised on his hips, head on the swivel. "Well, I think the books are a total loss," Dalton finally spoke up.

She followed his gaze. Half of an ancient oak tree stuck out of the ground, every branch bare. At the very top of it, she spotted the white truck panels nestled two stories in the air. The words Boris Brothers were upside down.

"I think you made the right call with the bolt cutters," she mumbled, arms closing around herself. Her body ached in ways it had never experienced before, and she wondered if everyone felt this way the morning after. They'd been awfully close to meeting their maker from the looks of it. But here they were, staring up at their transportation.

What were they gonna do now? No cars, no phones, and while the barn had been a life saver, she didn't fancy spending any longer in it than she had to. She glanced at Dalton, unsure what to say to him.

TWENTY

A **LARGE FARMHOUSE WITH** a wraparound porch and another barn was now easily visible behind them. One wall of a shed and its roof were collapsed between the two, and various detritus dotted the landscape. A pink flowered lawn furniture cushion floated in a puddle at the base of the porch stairs.

Dalton groaned, hooking his thumbs in the waist of his pants. "What do you say we try the house and confess our crime of cutting the locks and see if they have a phone."

She nodded mutely, following him as they walked deeper into the property. She stayed a half step behind him, eyes drawn to his backside. She knew what it felt like now. Knew how his muscles were tightening with each step. Knew what lay just beyond it.

And he knew all of her now, too. Neither had said a word about it. Why? Why hadn't he said a word? She had so many questions. Was she supposed to feel so raw all over? Supposed to be quite so distracted with every step reminding her of how she'd gotten to this state? Where was their back and forth? He had never been so quiet before. So far away. She glanced at his profile, wanting to interrogate him. But this wasn't the time, or the place.

Shame washed over her in the harsh light of day. All it had taken was a single kiss, and she'd shucked off years of preservation to give herself to the first person who had asked. Shoving the guilt down, she tightened her jaw.

Dalton gently knocked at the front door, standing a few feet back as they awaited an answer.

"It's got to be early," she mumbled.

"Round these parts it's just morning. Working farms have been up for hours by now," he explained.

An elderly woman greeted them, wiping her hands on a dish towel. "It's awfully early for a house call," she scolded.

Suddenly aware of her appearance, Analese combed her fingers through her unkempt hair, pulling a piece of straw from the back of it and dropping it on the porch. She studied her shoes, watching little muddy bubbles seeping from around the edges.

"I'm sorry to bother you," Dalton began. "We sort of got stranded in the storm last night and used your barn for shelter."

"You did?" she exclaimed, opening the screen door and looking in the direction of the barn. She pulled back, scanning them from head to toe.

"We did," he confirmed. "I'm afraid that's my truck up in the tree down there by the road." Dalton gestured over his shoulder.

"What in heaven's name?" The woman stepped out onto the porch, shielding her eyes and looking down the road. Her jaw hung open, and she clucked her tongue. "You were in that old barn all night?"

"If we'd had any other choice..." Dalton apologized.

"Don't you worry about it," she soothed. "I suppose you'll be wanting to use the phone. Come

222

on in." She walked ahead of them, one hand on the screen door till Dalton relieved her of the burden.

He nodded to Analese, who followed ahead of him into the woman's house.

"You must have been terrified. What were you kids doing driving around in this?"

"We were on our way back from Nashville," Dalton answered. "And the storm just came up out of nowhere."

"It was like the Spanish Inquisition," Analese added.

The woman chuckled taking Analese's hand. "Richard's out seeing what survived," the woman explained as she toddled ahead into the kitchen dragging Analese with her. "Wait till he sees you two." She chuckled at the words.

She pointed at the kitchen table and gestured for Analese to have a seat. "Got some coffee if you want."

"That would be magic," Dalton replied. "If it's not too much trouble."

She passed him a wireless phone from its base on the counter. "Young lady?"

"No thanks," Analese declined. She tried to ignore the scent of biscuits and gravy and spicy sausage that filled the air.

Dalton dialed the number quickly, turning his back to them.

"How'd you get into that barn? Richard lost the key to that rusty old lock a decade ago."

Analese hid her cringe, wondering what ancient dust had found its way into her sensitive places.

"Oh, Dalton's a maintenance man. He had some tools in the truck and was smart enough to take them with us when we went looking for shelter."

The woman's kind face frowned deeply. "You must've been terrified."

"Oh, we were fine."

"God's lookin' after the both of you. The fact that you found that driveway between the runoff ditches is a miracle all by itself."

"You have a beautiful estate," Analese complimented. "How long have you and Richard lived here?"

"Since the fifties. Raised three kids in this place. Now it's just us and the chickens. I'm hoping that old man of mine finds them. Lost all the new eggs last night."

"I'm so sorry. That's awful," Analese sympathized.

"Ah, that's all right. Critters have a way of finding their way home. It's still early."

Dalton wasn't on the phone long, passing it back to their hostess. "Our friend will be by as soon as he can to collect us."

"Have a seat," she invited. "How far did you have to go? Nashville's a trek from here."

"Down to Erin," Dalton replied, wrapping his large hands around the mug that she handed him next.

Analese watched his face relax as he inhaled the coffee.

"Well, your friend's gonna be a minute coming after you. You both need a good, hot meal and some dry clothes."

"Oh, that's too much," Analese protested.

"Nonsense. I can't have those muddy clothes dripping all over my kitchen. Take off those shoes and come back here to the washroom. I'll get you both a robe, and you just bring all that and put it in

225

the washer then you can eat. And if you need a shower, we got one of those too."

"That's not necessary," Dalton said.

"It is. It's the Christian thing to do," she insisted, grabbing Dalton's sleeve with two fingers.

Every last gangly inch of him stumbled after her.

"You too, Missy. Don't make an old lady drag you too."

Properly rebuked, Analese tiptoed behind them. The washroom was small containing an old top-load washer and dryer and a trio of cotton lines stretched across the length of the room. A faded green bathrobe hung from a hook with a quilted, flowered housecoat beside it.

"Don't dawdle. We'll get your clothes washed and dried before anyone can get here from Erin. Come back to the table and eat. I'm starting another batch of gravy for ya. I can whip up some grits too."

"No, ma'am. Really," Dalton insisted. "The biscuits and gravy are more than enough."

"You youngins. Won't let nobody spoil you no more. That's what's wrong with this generation," she grumbled. She reached for the doorknob. "I won't peak, I promise. You just come on out to the kitchen once that machine's running. Put those shoes in too."

Without another word, Analese was alone with Dalton in the cramped space. Sunlight beamed through the curtain at one end of the room, and Analese felt her face burning.

"I promise not to look either," Dalton swore as he reached for the green bathrobe.

"I knew you were going to stick me with the flowers," she teased.

"It goes perfectly with the hay sticking out of your hair."

She frowned, rolling her eyes then turned her back to him. Part of her wanted to watch him undress in the light. To lay her eyes over all the flesh she'd touched last night. But she wasn't ready to return the favor and instead put her back to him before stripping out of her clothes. Getting them off was far easier than putting them on, and she covered herself as quickly as she could in the zip-up temporary dressing gown.

"Are you decent?" she murmured as she gathered

her pile of clothes from the floor.

"Yeah," he replied softly.

She turned to see the lid to the machine open, and Dalton's underwear landed on top of the spindle in the tub. She chuckled. "Well, at least this isn't awkward. Not our first load of laundry together."

He quirked a smile and nodded, reaching for the laundry powder on the shelf above the machines. "Throw yours in, missy," he instructed.

She dropped her clothes in, trying not to think about being naked beneath the thin, borrowed outfit.

Dalton tugged at the tie on his robe and nodded toward the kitchen. "Let's go."

Their hostess was trotting between the stove, the sink, and the kitchen table. She paused to scrape the contents of a skillet into a giant white bowl with scalloped edges. "I just threw some biscuits back in the oven. They'll be ready in just a second. They're fresh this morning but left over from me and the hubby."

"That sounds amazing. Better than Shoney's," Dalton complimented, holding out a chair for

Analese.

"And I threw in a bit of bacon too. A little short on sausage, so the gravy's a bit thin."

"I'm sure it's perfect," Analese assured.

The back door in the kitchen swung open wide.

"Ethel, when did we get company?"

"Richard, these two weathered that horrible storm in that old barn of yours."

The elderly man shrugged off a canvas-style coat, its flannel lining sticking to his plaid shirt. "You don't say? I thought I saw that old door was open. Thought the storm did it."

"Well, technically, it did. With the help of a pair of bolt cutters. I'd be happy to reimburse you for the chain," Dalton offered.

"Nonsense. I lost that key so long ago I couldn't tell you what's in there anymore." He moved closer. "Richard," he introduced. He squeezed Dalton's hand and gestured to the sink. "This is Ethel."

"Dalton. And this is Analese."

They all shook hands, and Ethel pushed plates in front of them both. "What about the chickens?" she questioned.

"Myrtle and Bertha are in the barn. The others'll turn up," he assured. "Oh, and that gaggle of cats you like to feed are all hiding in the hayloft. One of 'em about took out my coat dropping down. I think they're hungry."

"I'll scrounge up something for them later. These two are a miracle. You see the truck in our tree down there?"

"Truck in a tree?" Richard repeated. "I'll be hog tied."

"I've already talked to my boss about it," Dalton explained. "He's working with the insurance company to get someone out here."

Ethel dropped a plate with half a dozen gorgeous biscuits on the table between them next to the gravy.

Dalton gestured for Analese to serve herself first while he continued talking to Richard about his conversation with Van. Analese watched him as their hosts sat down. He seemed just as at home as sitting in her mother's trailer. As though not one fiber of his being noticed they were sitting virtually naked in a stranger's kitchen.

The first bite of dough and creamy peppery gravy

warmed her from the inside out, and for the next several minutes, only food existed. The whole evening before had been a long, death-defying wait for this moment when her belly was full.

Dalton's brown eyes veritably sparkled as he and Richard debated the finer points of shoring up the barn. She couldn't have dreamed of the first man to take an interest in her to have handled it so perfectly. A part of her was proud to know he was the one to set the bar for her. Her family would love him.

Ethel darted from the table when the washing machine stopped, and in moments, the sound of the dryer tumbling their clothes punctuated their conversation. When a knock came at the front door, Analese swore she saw Richard and Ethel's smiles droop.

Dalton rushed to answer it, tightening his robe as he went. Analese looked at the washroom off the kitchen, wondering how wet their clothes were.

Van's voice carried from the porch all the way to the kitchen. "I knew you missed me, but this is a little extreme even for you."

"I'm just glad I got you and not Boris," Dalton

countered.

"I gotta send him pictures," Van replied, pulling out his cell. "Ain't nobody gonna believe me without 'em."

"You interested in a coffee, young man?" Ethel offered as Van followed Dalton to the table.

"Oh, thank you, but no. I have to get these two back before everyone starts writin' up their death certificates."

"You did actually find us stranded in a ditch," Analese replied.

Van chuckled. "I think I missed you." He looked from his friend to her and back. "Storm blow away your duds?" he questioned.

"No," Dalton replied. "Ethel refused to let us wait for you in soiled clothes. They should be out of the dryer any moment. I'm just gonna check their progress." Dalton and Van disappeared into the washroom, their voices too low to make out.

"Breakfast was delicious. I can't remember the last time I had anything as good," Analese praised.

Ethel's smile took over her whole face. "It was my pleasure."

The clothes were dry enough to get rolling, and Analese rushed to put her own clothes back on in the privacy of the back room. She hung the housecoat back on its hook beside the one Dalton had been wearing and rejoined the others as they were heading toward the front door.

"Thanks for looking after my friends," Van spoke up. "It was real Christian of ya, feeding and clothing them like that. We'll get that truck out of your way here soon."

"That would be great," Richard replied. "You take care getting back now."

They nodded, making their way out to Van's vehicle and piling in. "You fell into a pile of shit and came out like a pair of roses," Van noted.

Dalton chuckled. "Ana's my good luck charm."

From the back seat, she said nothing, turning her face to look out across the aftermath and hide the heat radiating from her cheeks. She looked back at the white truck in the sky.

"What about our phones and stuff?" she questioned, redirecting the conversation.

"It's gone," Van answered.

Through the back window, Analese eyeballed the ladder attached to the railings along the bed. "Is your ladder not tall enough?" she questioned.

Van snorted. "I'm not risking a half-ton pickup falling on my head because we climbed the tree. I'll run you by a phone store on the way home."

Analese cringed at the prospect of paying for a second new phone. She felt Van's gaze on her from the rear-view mirror and met his eyes.

"I'll put it on the company card since you were in a company vehicle," Van offered. "I won't feed you lemons without some sugar."

"Can you say it in a way that's less gross?" Dalton complained.

"What?" Van whined. "You don't want my sugar?"

Dalton answered by flicking his friend's ear.

TWENTY-ONE

STARING AT THE CEILING, Analese let another ring complete itself before she answered the cell phone. "Good morning, Martin. It's nice to hear from you."

"Nicer to hear from you. Van says you and Dalt almost met your makers on the drive home. Truck's up in some tree between here and home."

She closed her eyes. "So it is. But we're fine. Dalton's smart and a genius in a crisis."

"That boy's a godsend," Martin agreed.

"How are you feeling?"

"Pretty good. But I had an idea while I've been laid up in here, and it'll help me and you, I think."

At this, Analese sat up in bed. "Well, it's rude to keep a lady waiting," she teased. "Let's hear it."

"Well, I want to go home, but being so far away from the hospital, they don't want to let me go. And getting a home healthcare nurse doesn't suit the insurance company cause it's too far. I been talking to the nurses here, and they think if there was already a nurse dedicated to the area…a team of nurses for say, hospice care. Medicare will pay for it, but only in areas where it's convenient to them. Plenty of folks like me getting shipped away from their families so the insurance will cover it."

"That sounds disorienting to get taken away when you want your family the most," Analese sympathized.

"You know I don't take kindly to rentals, but you're in a bind, and I am too. If we rented out your trailer to folks for hospice, that would put nurses in the area. They'd qualify for the park regulations about home health care. I could get home tomorrow. The state foots the bill, the park gets regular medical assistance, and your property pays for itself. Feels like everybody wins."

Analese hummed at the prospect. "Will that work?"

"I think so. Looks like it on paper. Been talking to the folks that'd run the thing, and they seem pretty

236

motivated.”

She could go home. Wash her hands of her mother’s affairs and finally move on. “That is totally great with me.”

“It would mean you’d have to stay in touch with grouchy old me a bit longer.”

She giggled. “I think I can manage that.” In fact, now that she knew him, she’d miss Martin too when she left the area. Maybe having a few ties to Erin wasn’t a bad idea.

“And I’ll treat ya fair on the money,” Martin interjected stoically. “If there’s profit, I’ll share it with you.”

“I trust you, Martin.”

He grunted on the line. “Well, you did get it fixed up. They’ll send someone to inspect it when they bring me home. Make sure it’s fit for service.”

“Well, one person’s already died there, so I think it’ll do the trick.”

Martin laughed heartily until a cough took over. “Well, that’s a mite different than what we’re talking about now.”

“Of course,” Analese replied. “Do I need to stay

until you get back?"

He hacked a few more times before answering. "No. You've done your time. If you're ready, get on home, girl."

"Thanks, Martin."

"There's no thanks needed between friends."

Tears threatened to choke her suddenly, and she squeezed out her goodbyes as quickly as she could.

The light at the end of the tunnel wasn't a train after all. She might get through this unscathed.

But not unchanged.

Her life in Indiana could only have been described as stagnant. She was working a job she hated that barely paid the bills. Her life had been a vicious cycle of going through the motions. Of making sure everyone else was taken care of. When the call came that someone needed to close out her mother's "estate"…it was the natural assumption that she would be the one to stop what she was doing and handle it. Everyone else had a valid reason they couldn't do it.

Despite not loving her work, a pang of hurt lingered over the layoff. No matter how impersonal everyone said a layoff was, she knew she'd been selected over others who got to stay. And a solid paycheck was impossible to live without. She couldn't survive off the charity of strangers for long. Strangers like Dalton and Van and even Martin.

Dalton was on the brain again, and her mind immediately recalled their intimate moments. He was the only one who knew anything had changed. She couldn't say she felt different. She just knew more about the world — about herself.

The actual trauma of being where her mother had spent her final days had taken its toll. Seeing what Mary had been doing for decades on her own. None of it was a surprise. Not even the mice. But coming back to it after having sealed it out for so many years was like being thrown into a volcano as a sacrifice.

Her mother's community was vicious…full of malcontent and animosity. It was impossible not to be infected by it. And the emotions she had thought long buried since cutting her mother out of her life had bubbled toxically to the surface.

She needed a shower, some ibuprofen, and then she needed to get the heck out of Dodge. It was time to start over. Time to forget what anyone else thought about her. A new job meant she could be as outgoing or withdrawn as she liked. Maybe she wouldn't be the life of the party, but maybe it was time to be the host. To not just project confidence, but to actually be confident. To buy a new wardrobe. Well, maybe she could do that after the job started.

She took her time, drying her hair and styling it for the first time since she'd arrived. She picked out her best clothes and tucked the rest neatly into her travel bag. She piled her belongings near the front door, checking the place over one last time.

Everything was in order. If she started now, she could make it home in time for dinner if she only made minimal stops.

She pulled open the front door, surprised to see Dalton with one toe on the bottom step.

"Morning," he greeted.

She blinked in surprise, setting down her bags. "Hi." She stared, waiting for him to say more. But for the first time since they'd met, he seemed reluctant.

He eyed her feet. "Leaving?" he questioned.

She smirked, resting one hip on the door frame.

"No, I was just packing the car for any more emergencies."

"Smart," he replied, his mouth curled in a half smile. He tucked both hands into his back pockets before meeting her eyes. "Thought maybe we ought to talk. Didn't expect you to be headed out so soon."

Analese wanted to tell him that there wasn't anything in Erin for her, but the words died on her lips. If there was anything to keep her, it was over six feet tall and standing roughly three steps away. She stepped aside.

"Come on in," she welcomed.

Dalton hesitated briefly, and she scowled. Hadn't he come to her? Why was he hesitating now? He seemed to overcome the glitch in his stride and stepped past her, taking a seat at the kitchen table.

Wordlessly, she closed the door and took the seat opposite him. "If I'd have known you were coming, I'd have made some coffee."

He shook his head. "I don't need it. I just thought maybe we should talk after…the barn."

"Probably," she agreed.

Two days had passed since "the barn." She

hadn't known what to say the morning after. "Thank you," didn't seem appropriate, and their lack of any sort of relationship had precluded anything mushy that had occurred to her. After Van had carted them home, Analese had disappeared into the mobile home unit, and it had been radio-silent since.

For two days, she'd wallowed in bed torn between reliving the torrid event and telling herself it hadn't happened. One moment, she was wishing for Dalton beside her, and in the next, she was telling herself the whole thing had been so bad for him, he'd skipped town.

The conclusion she had come to before passing out the night before was that the sex, good or bad, had only been sex. It hadn't changed Dalton's world. It didn't matter that it changed hers. It wasn't going to happen again — or at least not with him.

All the waiting she'd done, dreaming of Mr. Right. Dreaming of the first time. Dreaming how much different and more mature she'd feel after the deed. And she still felt like the same, fledgling adult who was faking her way through life. Dalton hadn't said anything about the sex because it was over and done with.

She had evaluated and reviewed his every action from the time they'd gotten dressed till they'd arrived home. There had been no animosity. There had been some avoiding of eye contact. But his every action, while shy, seemed protective. Appreciative. Sex was just sex. A relationship it did not make.

She reflected on the event honestly. She'd liked it. Wanted more. And eventually, she would find someone she was willing to get naked for again. But it wasn't what defined her.

Even so, longing swirled in her belly as Dalton studied the tabletop. "That's not normal for me. One-night stands." He looked at her as the words left his lips.

"Me either," Analese answered softly. She laid her palms on the table to keep from crossing them instinctively over herself. She'd always read it made a person look closed off, and it was the last way she wanted to present herself in this moment.

"Well, you never..." he trailed off. He looked up from the table and met her eyes. "I don't really know what to say."

At least on this, they were on equal footing. An irrational urge to protect his feelings bubbled within her. "I'm not upset if that's what you're worried about," she excused. "I acted on my own free will."

"It felt that way," he noted. "I didn't know what you expected after."

"That makes two of us." She sighed. While she was planning to turn over a new leaf upon her return, she hadn't anticipated starting the transformation before she even started home. Adults could talk about sex without embarrassment. She struggled for words to describe it and let him off the proverbial hook. "It was beautiful, and life affirming, and I will always think about how perfect you were."

"Perfect?" he repeated, eyes focused on hers.

Analese swore his face turned red.

She shrugged. "As far as I know." Before he could protest, she added, "But I'm not expecting you to drop down on one knee and propose or anything. We barely know each other."

He nodded. "I've spent the last two days worried that you'd think I took advantage, or it was disappointing, or that I stole something from you that you weren't meant to give me."

"Disappointed?" she balked, then shook her head and shrugged. "I guess I could feel that way. But I don't."

He stared at his fingers, picking at one thumbnail. "And then I worried about you getting pregnant." This time, he turned purple.

She laughed. "At my age, I'm not sure that's much of a concern. But I guess it's possible." She patted his hand lightly. "And if it did, you'd be my first call to work it all out."

He smiled. "That's very fair of you." He glanced around the room.

"I don't get the impression that you're looking for a relationship."

He shrugged. "Well, no. I wasn't really."

Analese paused, mulling her thoughts slowly before speaking. She couldn't tell if he was trying to apologize, or if he was asking for more, or if he even cared the way he said so little.

She shook her head forgivingly. "We were alone in a barn, scared, and probably bored if we're honest," she excused. "I'm not holding you to it, and I don't regret it, either."

"I do like you, Analese," he breathed gently.

"I like you too, Dalton." As the words left her, her chest tightened. She felt like she had just trapped them both into a relationship. Was that what she wanted? To stay in Erin where her mother had died? To beg him back to Indiana? No. This was not what she meant. She did like him. But his admission had sounded more like platitude than sincerity. She had lived without him all this time. No need to complicate her life now when what she needed was a fresh start.

She pulled her hand from the table, resting it on the side of her neck and leaning nonchalantly on it. "Maybe if life had thrown us together differently…"

He stared.

Silence hung between them, and Analese looked at the doorway. She had been so close to getting away without this awkward conversation. She couldn't backtrack now. Adults had casual sex all the time and walked away from it. She could too.

After another minute, Dalton sighed softly. "Will you at least let me know you got home okay?"

There was her answer then. This was an apology. But she refused to be soured by the idea and offered a cheeky smile. "If you give me your number. Sure."

Dalton smacked his hand over his face then held it out for her phone.

"Of course." He added himself to her contacts then placed the phone on the table and stood. "Call if you get tired or…for any reason."

She joined him, holding her arms open for a hug. "One for the road?"

Dalton squeezed her tightly, then surprised her with a gentle kiss and one last hug.

"Good meeting you, Analese," he whispered against her ear.

He turned and let himself out before she could recover. She stood in the doorway, watching him climb into Van's usual truck.

"Thanks for everything, Dalton," she called.

He lifted a hand, then he was gone, leaves trailing after the back end of his vehicle.

She touched her lips. This had been an entirely different kiss than they'd shared in the barn. And for a moment, she wondered if she should call him back and never leave. This

   Instead, she gathered her bags, locked the door, and got behind the wheel of her car.

TWENTY-TWO

BY THE END OF EIGHT PLUS hours, restless didn't begin to describe how Analese felt. She'd made one pitstop five hours into her drive assuming that the last three hours would be a piece of cake. But it wasn't. Every restaurant, gas station, and shopping mall she passed called her name. The lights of major cities between Erin and South Bend begged her to stay a while. Stretch her legs. Do anything but stare at the endless stretch of highway before her.

Don't drink too much. You might have to stop.

Don't eat too much. You might gain weight.

Don't think about the people you left. You might turn around.

The exit for her street was like a welcome home banner, and the corners of her eyes were damp as she took a right at the light. Her compact car was loaded from bumper to bumper with anything she thought her family might want or be able to sell. But even the prize box of family photos sitting in the passenger seat beside her felt worthless. She'd rather have Dalton.

Usually when she drove long distances, she found a friend to call on the mobile phone. Time passed more quickly when chatting with a friend. But this trip, she'd made no calls at all.

She was afraid if she had, her new secret would come slipping out. She'd given herself to a man. Knew what everyone else knew. All the purity that had been shoved down her throat felt like propaganda. It felt hollow. It tasted like lies meant to control her.

No horror had befallen her after the giving. In fact, nothing had changed at all! No one looked at her differently. Her life wasn't in ruins. She had no drug or drinking habit to show for it. She simply knew what it felt like, and the world had kept turning.

A few more tears fell, and she growled at herself to stop this nonsense. *She* had made the decision to leave him behind. She should have pulled him into the bedroom and begged him to do it again, this time without the threat of a barn collapsing on top of them. To be slow and gentle, and to look at him while he touched her.

She mulled over their conversation that morning. He said he liked her. And she had boldly told him the truth. She liked him. Maybe it hadn't been a trap after all, but it was too late now. He was several states away already.

Upon their first meeting, he was not someone she thought she could ever be interested in, let alone get physical with. But after he'd rescued her so many times…treated her as an equal…as someone worthy of his time…it was the most obvious thing in the world.

She owed him so much.

The sight of her own front door should have delighted her. After weeks of trailer life, she was ready to get back to normal.

But what was normal now that she'd known and left Dalton?

She imagined him ducking in her front door…what he'd look like lounging on her hand-me-down couch. She could bring him sweet tea. She made a mean pitcher of tea.

Suddenly obsessed with the idea, she hurried to the kitchen, boiling a pot of water then tossing in a handful of teabags tied together. She watched as the water bubbled then foamed with a brown froth, the scent soothing her travel weary body. All the cups of tea she'd seen him drink floated in front of her closed eyes.

Maybe she couldn't have Dalton, but she could think about him whenever she wanted. It wasn't the sex that she missed. She missed the banter. She had never been so quick or witty before in her life. But when he was near, she was a woman. Independent.

She perched on the couch with a fresh cup of tea. It would have to do for now. There wasn't any other fresh food in the house, and her stomach grumbled in protest after driving so long without stopping. She considered ordering take out, but without a paycheck, it seemed frivolous. Grocery shopping would require emptying the car, which sounded like torture. And maybe she should let Dalton know she made it home okay. She had given her word to do so, after all.

Despite his offer to take her call at any time during her drive, she hadn't. What would she say? She was thinking about their naked time?

She tapped out a quick message. "The eagle has landed with no drama."

She watched for a response, but none came. He could be doing anything. Eating. Sleeping. Getting drunk with Van. He wasn't at her beck and call.

As soon as she set the phone down, it dinged with a response.

"It's a minor miracle. Glad you're safe."

She sighed, curling up into herself as she replied. "I know. I'm going to write it in my baby book. Which I found in Mary's trailer."

No further response arrived, and she tuned into whatever was on the television.

Her phone rang, and she answered it excitedly, hoping it was Dalton. However, the screen showed her brother's face smashed between his daughters.

"Sis, we drove by just to make sure the house was okay, and we saw your car! When did you get home?"

She forced disappointment out of her voice as she

answered. "Oh, not too long ago. Maybe going on an hour now?"

There was a mumbling in the background that was clearly his wife, Michelle. "I'm going to turn around and bring us back. You can't have any food in the house. Michelle suggested either pizza or Chinese. Our treat. And I haven't had Grand Wok in forever. They have the best hot braised beef."

"Oh, sweetheart," Analese protested. "I'm really very tired. I've been driving for eight hours. I can come to your place tomorrow and show you what I brought home." She could picture his wife badgering him from the passenger seat, and as much as she liked her sister-in-law, enduring the presence of anyone else at the moment was more than she could bear.

"It's no trouble," he insisted. "We're only ten minutes away."

"Thank you, but I'm fine. I've got ramen and some canned ravioli in the pantry. I won't starve," she insisted. "But I know you love the Chinese take-out around here. How about I call you tomorrow, and you can come over and help me unload the car, and we'll get Chinese then."

He laughed. "You know me so well. All right. I'll risk Michelle's wrath for you as long as you promise to call tomorrow."

"I will."

After hanging up, she went to peruse the aforementioned pantry. Piles of marked down canned goods and boxed dinners awaited her inspection, and for the briefest of moments, she cringed. It felt an awful lot like her mother's pantry had, sans bugs and mice infestations.

What was she stocking up for? The Zombie Apocalypse? A winter freeze in the middle of summer? She sighed. In the next few days, there was going to be a reckoning in her house-wide stashes, and some difficult decisions were about to be made.

A knock sounded at the door midway through shuffling around the boxed-dinners-shelf in the pantry.

Maybe her brother had dinner for one delivered in lieu of a visit. Who else would be knocking at ten p.m.? Could she get delivery this late? It had to be her brother or her father, she reasoned and trudged to the front door.

She should have looked through the peephole, but she didn't. She held it open far enough to poke her head around the edge to see who was disturbing the peace.

On *her* porch, in South Bend, Indiana, stood Dalton in all his trim, manly glory, wearing a pair of tight jeans beneath a loose-fitting T-shirt.

Analese threw the door wide, staring in shock. She pinched her forearm, yelping at the pain.

He spoke first, hands stuffed in his pockets. "I didn't think our conversation this morning was finished."

She blinked. "So you drove eight hours to finish?"

He shrugged. "Some conversations are best in person." He glanced at his feet then hers. "Can I come in?"

"Yes, of course," she replied, shaken from her stupor. She stepped aside, watching in wonder as his tall frame passed through the door. "How did you know where I live?"

"I got it from Martin," he replied. "Well, Van did. He just slipped right in the office and pulled it off the paperwork on his desk. It was very dramatic. Practically pushed me in the car and pressed the gas pedal."

She looked outside, seeing a silver sedan with Tennessee plates sitting behind her own. Even though she knew Dalton's truck was upside down in a tree the last she saw it, she hadn't considered that he might have another vehicle. Not that it mattered. Everything felt upside down.

She pressed the door shut. It was solid behind her, supporting her as she stared at him. Was this really happening?

As if sensing her thoughts, his palms cupped her cheeks. Her skin tingled at the contact, breath catching in her throat. He drew her closer, kissing her soundly. Analese gripped his arms for balance as she melted into him.

He nuzzled her face with his as he pulled away to catch his breath. "I should've said that," he murmured. "And said it till there was nothing else to say."

Licking her lips, Analese nodded. "I think you're right."

At this, Dalton wrapped her in his arms, kissing her thoroughly, bodies molding together.

She had thought of little else the entire drive home, and now that he was in her arms again, there was no time to waste. She slipped her hands beneath his shirt, running her palms first over his chest and then around back to his shoulders. Sneakily, she pressed her hands up, effectively separating them long enough to toss his shirt to the middle of the living room floor.

He chuckled. "Something's gotten into you," he teased.

"Not yet," she uttered, breathlessly, "but I'm trying very hard to make it happen."

He leaned in, kissing her neck just below the jawline, and she arched back to provide him access. His hands were on her waist, then under her shirt and shortly, her top matched his on the floor.

"I think it's time for the house tour, starting in the bedroom," he suggested.

"Absolutely," she agreed, taking him by the hand and tugging him up the stairs. "No time to waste. I hope you like Chinese and family, 'cause we've got about twelve hours till they descend on us."

"Us," he repeated, pausing at the top of the stairs. "I like that." He met her eyes, holding her gaze.

"Me too," Analese agreed, then dragged him to her bedroom.

THE END

ABOUT THE AUTHOR

Laura Christian was raised in St. Louis, MO but now resides in the great state of Texas with her husband, a Siamese cat, and a Jack Russel Terrier. In her spare time, Laura enjoys reading, sewing, knitting, painting, and mostly playing Fortnite with her besties.

To learn more about the author and other publications, visit http://www.thelaurachristian.com for more details.

OTHER PUBLICATIONS

Coming Attraction
Published 2022

Balancing the Scales
Published 2023

Grace Notes
Published 2024

Rae of Sunshine
Published 2024